"Are we going to break up?" Aaron said. "After all we've been through? Over *Mia*?"

Claire was silent. Did she want to break up with Aaron? Did she want to lose him again? Why had she gotten all dressed up and come here tonight if not to fight for him?

"That's up to you," she said at last.

"What do you mean?"

"The world is full of Mias," Claire said. "Can you promise me that you'll give this one up? And the next one? And the one after that?"

Aaron hesitated.

It was unbelievable, but he hesitated. It wasn't very long, but Claire imagined she could feel the planet turning slowly while she waited for him to speak.

"Of course I can—" he began, but she cut him off.

"Your silence is very articulate."

"Claire—"

She turned and began walking. As she passed the doorway she noticed Mia silhouetted there. Claire didn't care. She was finished with Mia. She was finished with both of them.

MAKING OUT #21

# Trouble with Aaron

## KATHERINE APPLEGATE

AN AVON FLARE BOOK

This is a work of fiction. Names, characters, places, and incidents either are the product of the author's imagination or are used fictitiously. Any resemblance to actual events, locales, organizations, or persons, living or dead, is entirely coincidental and beyond the intent of either the author or the publisher.

AVON BOOKS, INC.
1350 Avenue of the Americas
New York, New York 10019

Copyright © 1997 by Daniel Weiss Associates, Inc.,
and Katherine Applegate
Published by arrangement with Daniel Weiss Associates, Inc.
Library of Congress Catalog Card Number: 99-95192
ISBN: 0-380-81310-6
www.avonbooks.com/chathamisland

First Avon Flare Printing: February 2000

AVON FLARE TRADEMARK REG. U.S. PAT. OFF. AND IN OTHER COUNTRIES, MARCA REGISTRADA, HECHO EN U.S.A.

Printed in the U.S.A.

WCD   10  9  8  7  6  5  4  3  2  1

For my dad, who was so understanding about the snow tires—and everything else.

# Zoey

What kind of girlfriend flies off to Washington to attend a stupid conference the day after her boyfriend's father dies?

Don't answer that.

And how would I have felt if Lucas had hightailed it right in the middle of all that stuff with Mom and Dad?

Don't answer that, either.

But here I am, my suitcases packed so tightly that it'll probably create a black hole, and a plane ticket in my hand, and it sure seems like I'll be getting on a flight to Washington tomorrow.

But . . . how can I? Lucas needs me. He must need me. Even if you're not

close to your father (and
Lucas was about as far
away from his father as
you can be and still live
in the same house), it must
be horrible to lose him.

But . . . Lucas says I
should go. It's an honor,
it's a great opportunity,
it's not forever, blah,
blah, blah. Besides, I've
asked Nina and Benjamin
to take extra-good care of
him, so . . . so what? Does
that mean I'm not leaving
him when he needs me
most?

But Lucas has to work
on his father's fishing
boat, for the rest of the
summer at least. Maybe
it'll be easier if I'm not
around, distracting him
and making him feel guilty
for not spending more time
with me?

I should go.

I shouldn't go.

I feel like I could fill the rest of this notebook with those two sentences and still be writing them over and over, on the desk, on the floor, on the walls, when Lucas comes to pick me up and take me to the airport. . . .

# One

The idea had been for Zoey to fly out of Logan Airport in Boston, and that way she and Lucas would have an extra three hours together while he drove her there, hours to fill with talking and laughter and tenderness.

That had been the *idea,* Zoey reminded herself. But it hadn't exactly worked out that way. Instead it was more like two people who wind up sitting next to each other on a bus, both secretly wanting to read their paperbacks but feeling obligated to make conversation.

Zoey supposed this was mainly her fault. It seemed like every sentence out of her mouth began with, "In Washington . . . ," or even worse, "In California . . . ," and each time Lucas gave her a reproachful look.

And she wondered if Lucas really needed to be making a six-hour drive today, when tomorrow he would have to be up at dawn to work on the boat. She glanced at him. He had dark circles under his eyes, and his wonderful blond hair hung lank and lifeless. Zoey sighed. This drive had been a bad idea, and now it was nearly over. They were only a mile or so from Logan Airport.

"So, um, listen," she said softly, touching Lucas's arm. "I'm sure Nina and Benjamin will—will hang out with you a lot."

4

They passed a sign for the airport, and Lucas eased the car into the exit lane. "Great," he said under his breath. "When *I* go away, I'll be sure that *you're* baby-sat by my brother and my best friend."

"You don't have a brother," Zoey teased.

"Or a best friend," Lucas muttered.

Zoey swallowed and stared out the window. A minute later they were following the signs for departing flights. Zoey looked up in surprise as they passed a sign for short-term parking.

"Don't you want to—" she began.

Lucas pulled the car to such an abrupt halt at the curb that she had to brace her arm against the dashboard. He threw the car into park and unbuckled his seat belt.

"Don't you want to come inside?" Zoey asked. She hated the pleading tone in her voice, but she couldn't seem to stop herself.

Lucas was already out of the car, lifting her heavy suitcases onto the sidewalk.

"Lucas, my plane doesn't leave for another hour and a half," Zoey said.

Lucas slammed the trunk shut. "I know, but it's another three hours back for me," he said stonily.

*Is this really Lucas?* Zoey thought crazily. *Is this really the person I love?*

"Well, I—if you think—if you want—" she floundered. She stood on the sidewalk next to her bags, amid the roar of cars, with frantic people rushing by her. A hot rush of exhaust fumes creased the cream-colored linen jacket she was wearing. She had chosen this outfit with so much care, wanting to look cool and sophisticated as she arrived in Washington and yet fresh and sexy when she said good-bye to Lucas. But all she felt now was hot and wrinkled—and abandoned.

"Lucas—" she began again, but he merely bent his head and kissed her. And Zoey felt—even hurt and confused—the same thrill she felt every time he kissed her.

She tried to hold him. "I love you," she whispered.

A horn honked, and Lucas disengaged himself from her. He gave her an awkward wave and got in the car. Zoey watched in disbelief as he put the car in gear and drove out into the airport traffic. It wasn't possible. Lucas was leaving her, without spending the last-possible minute with her? Without saying he loved her?

"Hey, miss, you need help with those bags?"

Zoey turned. A porter was looking at her irritably.

"No, thanks," she murmured. "I can manage." She picked up a suitcase in each hand and began struggling forward. Not only were her suitcases incredibly heavy, she was having difficulty seeing through her tears. She stumbled and twisted her ankle in her stupid cream-colored pumps. The tears were flowing freely now.

She felt someone tugging at one of her bags. *The porter,* she thought dismally, *and I have no idea what to tip him, and he'll probably yell at me.*

But it wasn't the porter, she realized suddenly. At least she hoped it wasn't, because he'd set down the bags and wrapped his arms around her from behind.

"I'm sorry," Lucas whispered into her hair. "I'm sorry, and I love you, too, and I'm just being selfish by not wanting you to go, and I would love to come into that airport and buy you a cup of coffee, and wait at the gate with you, and be the last person waving as your plane takes off."

"Lucas," Zoey whispered. She turned around and hugged him, kissing his neck. "Should I stay?"

He squeezed her tight for a moment. "No," he said at last. "You go, but come back to me."

6

"Oh, yes," Zoey said against his chest.

Lucas picked up both her suitcases in one hand—*I must have really weak arms*, Zoey thought—and slipped his free hand around her waist.

"Come on," he said, leading her toward the glass doors. "Did I ever tell you about the time I sat next to this woman on a plane who offered me $175 to jump out of a cake at her bachelorette party?"

Zoey laughed. "Why $175?" she asked. "Why not just go up to two hundred dollars?"

"She said I'd make more in tips," Lucas said with a straight face.

Zoey laughed harder and stood on tiptoe to kiss him. She wondered if it was possible to miss someone while you were still with them, before you even said good-bye.

Claire Geiger stepped off the ferry and onto the landing. She stopped to adjust one of her sandals, and her long black hair fell forward across her face. She wore a simple red T dress, but it clung to her figure so perfectly that she looked as though she'd walked off the cover of *Teen People* or *Seventeen*. One of the "Summer's Here" issues.

"Wait up, Claire!" a voice called, shattering the image. "I have the name of that dermatologist you wanted!"

Claire didn't even glance up as her sister, Nina, fell into step beside her.

"Seriously," Nina continued in a loud voice. "He can really help with those blemishes."

Claire shot her a withering look. "To what do I owe this honor?"

Nina looked a little evasive. She had the ever-present unlit Lucky Strike between her lips, and her spiky hair and dark lipstick were as vibrant as ever, but Claire thought she detected something distracted and nervous in her sister's gray eyes. "What honor?"

"Well, I don't think we've walked home from the ferry together since . . ." Claire frowned. "I don't think we've *ever* walked home from the ferry together."

"You're forgetting the time I had a sprained ankle," Nina said.

Claire looked puzzled. "Why? Did we walk together then?"

"Of course! You carried my books every day for two straight weeks!"

"I did?"

"Wasn't that you?" Now Nina looked confused. "Oh, no, it was Zoey. Wow, how'd I ever make that mistake? Even for a minute, even for a *second*—"

"Okay, okay," Claire said irritably. "You still haven't said why you're walking with me today—"

She broke off as she saw Benjamin walk by. He waved, and the girls waved back at him. Claire looked at her sister and saw a sad expression beneath the cheerful smile.

"Oh, I get it," she said. "You'd rather walk with me than risk having Benjamin *not* walk with you."

Nina's eyes were still following Benjamin as he went up the street in that odd, hurried walk he'd had ever since he'd gotten back his sight, like there wasn't time enough to do and see everything he wanted to. And, Claire supposed, maybe there wasn't. Eight years was a very long time to be blind.

Nina sighed wistfully. "I just—we just—we haven't been getting along lately," she said weakly. "Well, that's kind of an understatement, I guess, but I just don't want another argument."

8

Claire groaned inwardly. Not only did she have to walk with Nina; now she had to listen to the Lonely Hearts Club woes. "Listen, I told you a long time ago, just be direct with Benjamin," she said. "Just talk to him about whatever's bothering you."

"Yeah, well, ideally speaking, when I talk, I like the other person to listen," Nina said. "Maybe even talk back to me. And these days Benjamin doesn't stay in one place long enough."

"He's going through a big transition—"

"Yeah, yeah, I know," Nina said, suddenly impatient. She changed the subject. "So where were you, anyway?"

"At the mall," Claire said. "Buying stuff for next year."

"Oh, of course," Nina said. "Wonderful next year, when everyone moves away and abandons me."

Claire decided she was just as glad that Nina never had walked home with her before. "Where were you?" she asked.

"I was at the mall, too," Nina said, sighing. "Applying for a job at the Earring Hut. I saw it advertised in the paper."

"Did you get it?"

Nina shook her head. "Actually, I didn't even finish filling out the application because right in the middle of it, I remembered how last year on television they interviewed some poor girl who worked at the Earring Hut. And this girl was going on and on about the Christmas rush and her face was all kind of shiny and she looked really overworked and I had this sudden fear that I would still be working there at Christmas and it would be me on television, saying, *Yeah, there's been a big demand for hoops and—*"

Claire snapped her fingers in front of Nina's face.

"Nina, it's okay. That was just some sick fantasy, all right?"

"It was incredibly realistic," Nina said doubtfully.

They were in front of the Geigers' large house, and Nina stopped to pull the usual assortment of bills and magazines out of their mailbox.

"Bill, bill, bill," she said, flipping through the letters. "How come nobody ever writes me? Bill, flier, bill, hey"—she tossed a white envelope at Claire—"your coven is having its annual membership drive, I see, and—oh, no! Dad's AmEx bill!"

Claire glanced at her envelope. There was no return address or postmark, just her name written in block letters. She slid her finger under the flap. "What's so alarming about Dad's AmEx bill?"

"The bazillion things I charged to it," Nina said, looking dismayed. "Including three water taxi rides."

"Nina!"

"I know. . . . What should I do, burn it?"

Claire shook her head. "He'll just ask them to send another."

"Hey!" Nina brightened. "I can make strawberry shortcake. That's his favorite, and he loves it when either one of us gets all feminine and domestic."

"Nina, do you really think strawberry shortcake is going to—" But Nina was already sprinting across the yard and into the house, presumably to get to work in the kitchen.

Claire ripped open her envelope and pulled out a Polaroid snapshot. She frowned at it. The snapshot was too blurred and out of focus to tell what it was. It looked like an extreme close-up of a candle. Why would someone be sending it to her?

She turned it over and froze. On the back of the photograph, in the same block lettering as on the envelope, someone had written: *Wait*.

For a moment it seemed as though the bright afternoon grew cooler. Claire nearly shivered. She looked around her suddenly, twisted her neck to take in the neat green lawns and colorful flower beds and immaculate houses all at once.

But the street was empty.

# Two

Nina was so anxious to give her father the impression of being sweet and feminine that she actually put on a dress. Nobody knew she owned the dress, not even Zoey. Nina'd bought it from a thrift shop in Weymouth. The saleslady had told her it was a flapper's dress from the 1920s. Well, Nina had some doubts about that. She supposed a *real* flapper's dress would probably cost lots more than this dress, which only cost nine dollars. Nina suspected that she was probably wearing someone else's old Halloween costume.

Still, as she surveyed herself in the mirror, she was kind of pleased. The dress was bright blue and beaded, with a high but soft neckline that Nina liked. She thought it suited her short hair. Not everyone could wear a dress like this. Not—not Claire, for instance. But it suited Nina, suited her erratic style.

She twirled suddenly, listening to the beaded fringe rattle pleasantly. She paused for a moment. It wasn't her father who she wanted to see her in this dress. She scampered down the hall and picked up the upstairs phone extension. She dialed a number she'd had memorized since early childhood.

"Hello?"

"Benjamin? It's me."

"Well, hi, you," his voice came down the line, thrilling her. She loved talking to him on the phone. It was almost like old times, when he was blind. *I can't believe I would even think that,* Nina thought disgustedly. *I am the worst person who ever lived.* She cleared her throat and hurried on.

"I was wondering if you would like to come over for dinner tonight?" she said. Her voice rose embarrassingly on the last word. All alone in the upstairs hall, she blushed. Was this her boyfriend or what? Why was she so nervous?

"Why?" Benjamin asked.

*Why?* Nina thought hysterically. *Do I need a reason? Because I want to see you, you dork! Because I would see you every single second if I could! Because I'm in love with you!*

But she said none of these things. Instead she faltered and said, "Well, because I made this strawberry shortcake and—"

Benjamin interrupted her by groaning. "Oh, no, you're not trying the Betty Crocker routine on your father again, are you? What happened, the phone bill came today?"

Nina bristled. "No, the phone bill did not come today," she said shortly.

But Benjamin wasn't fooled in the slightest. "Well, what, then? The Visa or something? It's a good thing your dad doesn't have a tendency toward strokes or heart attacks. What am I saying?" He interrupted himself. "You and Claire are probably *giving* him high blood pressure by running up his credit cards all the time."

"Benjamin—"

But he was too hyper to stop and listen. "One day someone will find him lying dead by the mailbox, his

13

brains smoking, an open MasterCard bill clutched in his hand—"

"Look," Nina said furiously, "do you want to come or not?"

Benjamin ignored her tone. "Hmmm," he said. "Do I want to see poor Mr. Geiger's blood pressure jump another twenty systolic pressure points—"

Nina felt as though her own blood pressure had just increased by at least a hundred points. Did Benjamin want to come to dinner or didn't he? Why was he toying with her in this insulting way? She wasn't—she wasn't the Avon lady calling. (Although would Benjamin toy with an Avon lady? She brushed the question aside.)

"Benjamin," she said slowly, her every word as crisp as bacon, "do. You. Want. To. Come. To. Dinner."

"Actually I can't," Benjamin said. "I'm making sweet-and-sour pork for my parents. It's something I've discovered I love doing. Me—cooking!" He sounded so happy. "Can you imagine? It used to be all I could do to heat up a can of soup. I remember this one time I poured applesauce all over my mashed potatoes because my mother had put the applesauce in the gravy boat and . . ."

But Nina wasn't listening anymore. Benjamin had made dinner—his first dinner, a big festive occasion, and he hadn't invited her? He hadn't even *thought* to invite her? Even now he wasn't thinking of it! How much effort would it take for him to say, *Why don't you come over here for dinner, Nina? I want you to see what a great cook I am. . . .*

She swallowed. "Well, in that case," she said brightly, not even finishing her sentence. In that case—what? "I'd better go. The strawberries are burning."

*"The strawberries are—"*

"I mean, the shortcake. It's burning," she said

hastily. "Good-bye, I'll talk to you later." She let the receiver drop into the cradle with a satisfying thunk.

She drifted slowly down the hall to her room. The blue flapper dress now seemed to be making an annoying clatter instead of a pleasing clink. She caught sight of herself again in the mirror. She'd been wrong before. The dress was too bright, too garish. Thank goodness Benjamin hadn't seen her in it! It would have blinded him all over again.

Suddenly the dress felt terribly confining. Too tight, too stiff, even scratchy. She tore at the zipper furiously, and the fragile beaded material tore with a ragged rustling noise. Nina didn't care. She tore the dress off as though it were suffocating her and threw it savagely into her wastebasket, pounding it down with her foot until it was nothing more than a small pile of bright blue glitter.

Kate sat in the window seat of her bedroom, watching the traffic go by—if you could call two little kids on bicycles and one old man on foot *traffic*.

She was still wearing her pajamas, even though it was late afternoon, and her lovely red hair lay against her scalp in sweaty rust-colored ringlets. Kate frowned. Why hadn't she taken a shower today? She supposed it hadn't seemed worth the effort. Or else time had gotten away from her. That seemed to happen more and more, time getting away from her. And yet she couldn't exactly say what she did all day.

Take today, for example. She'd slept late. She'd looked through a lot of catalogs. But when she'd finally decided what she wanted, a beautiful blue velvet jacket from J. Crew, she couldn't find the energy to pick up the phone and place the order. Then lunch. Kate hadn't had much of an appetite these days, but she'd been watching TV—oh, hey! There was something else she'd done today. She'd watched a rerun of *Baywatch*—and she'd seen a commercial for pizza, and suddenly she'd been hungry for pizza: spicy, steaming hot, lots of pepperoni. But ordering a pizza would have meant calling Passmores' Restaurant and making conversation over the telephone with Mr. or Mrs. Passmore and then making actual person-to-person conversation with Christopher when he delivered it, and—well, she just hadn't felt up to that.

Instead she'd rummaged around in the kitchen and eaten almost a whole entire pan of lasagna. Probably someone had brought it over for the funeral. She'd only meant to cut herself a single piece, but somehow she'd eaten her way through most of it, and then, well, it hadn't seemed worth saving just a piece and a half, so she ate that, too.

*I'm going to get fat,* Kate thought ruefully, looking down at her pajama-clad body. *I can't eat a whole pan of lasagna and not do any exercise.* Exercise, that would probably make her feel better. She could put on some shorts, jog around the island, sweat all the toxins out of her body while the salty breeze blew all thoughts of her mother out of her head—all the thoughts of her mother and her mother's weary voice. *Kate, I know you like this little place, but you're not doing well. You're acting just like you did before. . . .* But even as Kate thought it, she knew she wouldn't go jogging. It would be like everything else—not worth the effort in the end. Why did she feel like this? Maybe a nap would—

She spotted a familiar figure on the street. Jake! She cringed against the curtains, touching her greasy hair with her fingertips. She couldn't let him see her like this. And her face would be all blotchy and shiny from the lasagna, too. Well, thank heavens, she was the only one here. Mrs.

Cabral was at the airport, either taking some relatives there or picking up a new bunch. And Lucas wasn't back from taking Zoey to the airport. Well, good. There'd be nobody to open the door and say, *Hi, Jake. Why don't you go on up; I'm sure she'd love to see you. . . .*

The doorbell rang. Kate leaned her head forward until her forehead was resting against the glass and she could just see Jake standing on the porch.

The doorbell rang again.

*If he rings one more time, I'll answer,* Kate told herself. *He's seen me in pajamas before.*

But Jake seemed to figure there was no one home. He walked back to the street. If he looked up, he would see Kate.

*Come on, look up,* Kate thought. *See me. That way, I'll have to come down. You make the decision for me, Jake.*

Jake hesitated, as though he'd heard her. He kicked at the ground absently with one foot, hesitating. Then he began walking in the direction of the ferry.

Kate sat back. She felt let down. But that was dumb. Jake thought no one was home. She hadn't answered the door. What was he, a mind reader?

What she should do was take a shower, slip on a sundress, and go meet the next ferry. Jake would be thrilled. They could go out, take a walk, watch TV together. . . .

Kate sighed. She knew that this wouldn't happen any more than she would go jogging. She stood up wearily and walked over to her bed, stepping over the empty lasagna pan. She needed to take that to the kitchen, along with all the dirty glasses scattered around the room. Well, she'd do that later.

She slid between her sheets. Sleep didn't come immediately. After all, Kate had already slept for thirteen hours. But she closed her eyes and concentrated, and ten minutes later she was dreaming.

# Three

Aaron Mendel lay on his bed at his friend Andy's house, listening to a Blur CD. He was wearing a white T-shirt and tan shorts. His dark hair was curly and ingenuously rumpled. His eyes, blue without a touch of hazel, were distant. He was thinking about Claire.

He liked to picture her in one particular pose: bending forward to straighten her miniskirt, her dark hair tousled and half covering her face. Other people might admire Claire's style and cover girl looks, but Aaron liked her best when she wasn't so perfectly put together.

He wanted to go see Claire right now, right this minute, but going to his mother's house had become a drag lately. She and Burke disapproved of him and Claire being together to such an extent that it was like trying to have a relationship in a house where every room was bugged. Worse, actually. Even when he and Claire weren't doing anything, even when they were sitting around talking about what to watch on TV, his mother or Burke always burst in, looking apprehensive. It was so much easier to crash with friends on the mainland and only go to his mom's place every fourth night or so. And now that Andy, one of the other band members, was in town, he hardly went back at all.

Andy knocked and poked his head around the door.

"Call for you," he said, holding out the cordless phone.

Aaron hoped it was Claire. "Hello?"

"Hi, Aaron." It was Mia. Aaron had dated her for a couple of months last year, and then at his mother's urging, he'd called her up again a week ago and they'd gone to see a movie together.

"Oh, hi."

"Were you expecting someone else?"

"No . . . no. How are you, Mia?"

"Missing you. Have you had dinner yet?"

"No," Aaron said before he thought.

"Good," Mia said promptly. "Do you like Mexican food?"

"Well, yeah. Sure."

"Great. Because I'm making enchiladas, and you're going to want to marry me when you taste them."

Aaron cringed a little. Claire would never hint like that. Claire would never fix anyone dinner, for that matter. Claire would let other people do the fixing.

"Mia, I don't think that's such a good idea," he said.

"Why not?"

"Well, because I just saw you a day or so ago. You know that I—that *we* see other people."

"Sure," Mia said easily. "But we could still have dinner. People who see other people still have dinner. People who barely know each other have dinner."

Aaron almost said yes. But the problem was that he knew dinner wasn't all Mia was offering. It might start out as dinner, but . . .

"I just don't think it's a good idea," he said. And then, to soften his words, he added, "Not tonight, at least."

"Okay," Mia said. "Call me."

"I will."

"Promise?"

"Promise."

19

"Bye."

Aaron hung up. One battle won. He loved Claire. He wanted to be faithful to her. Still, the idea of Mia stayed with him. Her and her dinner invitations and her easy willingness . . .

"Andy?" Aaron called suddenly.

Andy reappeared in the doorway. "Yeah?"

"Feel like going out for a pizza?"

"Sure."

Aaron stood up, feeling relieved. It was always better to be on the safe side.

The moonlight was wobbling on the surface of Big Bite Pond as Aisha strolled around it. Aisha held on to Christopher's hand. Kendra held his other hand. Aisha liked the familiarity of this. She and her fiancé and her future sister-in-law. She only hoped it would stay the way it was now—peaceful and happy. Christopher was trying to give Aisha and Kendra a chance to get to know each other. But Aisha could tell that he still felt tense about allowing her this glimpse into his past. Now that Aisha was spending time with the two of them, it seemed that Christopher blew up at Kendra at the slightest excuse.

"So what are we doing tomorrow?" Kendra said.

"*We* have to earn some money," Christopher said. Aisha held her breath, but his voice sounded pleasant enough.

The idea popped into Aisha's head and out her mouth so quickly, she was almost surprised to hear it. "If you'd like to make a little money, Kendra," she said, "I'm sure I could find you work in my parents' B&B."

"Hey, that would be great," Christopher said.

Kendra wrinkled her nose. "I don't know."

Aisha saw Christopher's brow darken, and she jumped in before he could speak. "It would just be for

20

a day or two, sort of on a trial basis," she said, secretly hoping her father would agree to this. "You know, you could see how much you liked working for my parents, my parents could see how much they, um, liked you." Aisha was sorry she'd put it that way because she had a feeling her parents *wouldn't* like Kendra working for them. She didn't seem like an especially hard worker. Well, she'd cross that bridge when she came to it.

Kendra still looked unconvinced. "What time would we start?" she asked in the same sort of tone she might use to ask if the job required handling raw fish.

But Christopher obviously thought Kendra was saying, *Great! What time do we start?* because he dropped both of their hands and put his arms around their shoulders, squeezing. "Cool," he said. "That will help solve a lot of problems. Thanks, Eesh." He gave her shoulders another squeeze.

Kendra, on the other hand, looked like someone who had just inadvertently offered to pay for dinner. "Wait a minute," she said, panic mounting in her voice. "I haven't agreed to anything."

"Oh, that's right," Christopher said sarcastically. He dropped his hands from their shoulders. "You agreed to live in my apartment and eat my food and talk for ungodly long periods of time long-distance on my telephone. The only thing you haven't agreed to is paying your share. So I've just agreed for you. And Aisha was kind enough to offer you this job out of the blue. So you either show up bright and early tomorrow morning or you can haul your ass right back to Boston."

There was a moment of heavy silence. Kendra shot Christopher a murderous look, and her beautiful lips turned pouty.

Aisha walked along numbly, shocked that Christopher could speak so harshly to his sister. It wasn't that Aisha

21

couldn't understand brother-sister feuding. She herself often thought that she would cut off her pinky finger if it meant that she never had to see her brother, Kalif, again. But that was different. For one thing, Kalif was younger than she was. She had hoped by the time she and Kalif were the same age as Christopher and Kendra, they would be past all that. It was also different because Kendra was smart and beautiful and friendly (if a little irresponsible and whiny) and Kalif was, well, *Kalif.*

Impulsively she reached across Christopher to touch Kendra's hand. "It'll be fun," she said softly, sincerely. "I'll be working with you. You can tell me all sorts of embarrassing things about Christopher."

Kendra laughed, her good humor restored. "What do you want to know?"

Aisha's hand found Christopher's in the dark, and she pressed it reassuringly. "Um, what was his first word?"

"She won't know that. She's younger than I am," Christopher said morosely, but he didn't sound as angry as he had a minute ago.

"I do so know," Kendra said. "It was *girl.*"

Aisha laughed and was surprised at how natural the laugh sounded, how natural it *felt.* She was suddenly optimistic. She would bring Christopher and Kendra together through the sheer force of her determination. She would get to the bottom of whatever problems lay between them. "What a surprise," she teased Christopher gently, and he rewarded her with a faint smile. "Tell me something else," she said to Kendra.

"Like what?"

"Well, what did he wear to the prom? Was it one of those baby blue tuxedos?"

"Prom?" To her surprise, both Christopher and Kendra laughed. "Our school didn't have a prom," Christopher said.

"What do you mean? All schools have proms."

"Not schools that can barely afford books," Christopher said, and Aisha's cheeks flushed. It was hard to remember how different Christopher's background was from her own.

Kendra came to her rescue by continuing merrily. "Anyway, if we had had a prom, Christopher wouldn't have made it on time because he would have been home blow-drying his hair."

"He didn't!" Aisha said, half in mock horror, half in real horror.

"Kendra," Christopher said warningly.

"Honest to God," Kendra said. "I think he wanted it to, like, *feather* or something, which is basically impossible—oh, hey, yikes!"

Christopher had swept Kendra up in his arms and was running toward Big Bite Pond.

"It's true!" Kendra called over his shoulder. "I have the pictures to prove it."

"That does it!" Christopher yelled. "I'm throwing you in."

He walked out on the tiny little dilapidated deck that stood on the far side of the pond. Kendra was shouting and beating at him with her fists. Aisha just watched, shaking her head and smiling.

Christopher held Kendra's slender body out over the water. "Promise," he said. "Promise to keep your mouth shut."

Kendra was struggling so much, Aisha thought she might wind up in the pond even if Christopher didn't drop her. "I promise!" she screamed. "Anything! Whatever you want!"

Christopher set her carefully on the dock beside him. "Good," he said. "The past is the past. Make sure it stays that way."

# Four

"Hello?"

"Lucas? It's me."

"Zoey! How was your flight?"

"Um, okay. I sat next to a brand-new doctor."

"What do you mean, brand-new?"

"I mean, he'd been a doctor for about five minutes. He was flying home from graduation."

"Oh . . . did he try to make a pass at you?"

"No. He tried to take my blood pressure, though. But I guess he wasn't very expert at it because according to him, I don't have any circulation."

"Anything else?"

"Well, he wanted to use his stethoscope, but I drew the line."

"No, I mean anything else going on? How's Washington?"

"Oh, Lucas, it's wonderf—I mean, it's okay. Nothing special."

"Zoey, it's okay to like Washington. I *want* you to like it. I want you to have a wonderful time."

"I guess. . . . But Lucas, you know what?"

"What?"

"They said that one student is going to be chosen to

24

stay on an extra week. But I wouldn't even want to or anything. It's just that—"

"You're a shoe-in, Zoey. And I want you to stay as long as you can and get as much out of it as you can."

"OK. But I miss you already."

"Me too."

"Good night."

"Good night. I love you."


"Hello?"

"Claire?"

"Yes?"

"It's me."

"Who?"

"Aaron."

"Aaron who?"

*"Claire."*

"I thought you were going to call me earlier."

"I was out."

"With Lindsay?"

"That's over. I told you. I was out having a pizza. With Andy."

"Oh."

"What have you been doing?"

"Washing my hair."

"Oh."

"That's a joke. Listen, when do you want to come see me?"

"Tomorrow?"

"Sounds good. I'll see you when I see you, then."

"You don't beat around the bush much, do you?"

"I'm trying to free up the line so my boyfriend can call me."

"Claire?"

"Hmmm?"

"I love you."

"I know you do."


"Aisha?"

"Oh, hey . . ."

"I thought we'd never be alone together."

"We never *were*."

"Well, we're alone now, in a way."

"I suppose."

"Want to have phone sex?"

"Not really. I'm on the kitchen phone. My dad might come down for a glass of milk."

"He doesn't drink milk. He has lactose intolerance."

"How do you know that?"

"Trust me, I know."

"Okay, well, what are you wearing?"

"Eesh? I love you."

"I love *you*."

"I miss *you*."

"I miss *you*."

"Gross! Could you guys at least go back to phone sex?"

"Kendra! Put the phone down. *Right now!*"

"Hey, no need to shout. I was trying to call the time lady."

"Kendra, I'm warning you."

"Look, it's a free country—"

*Sounds of scuffle.*

"Christopher? Christopher? Kendra? Anyone?"


"Hello?"

"Kate?"

"Hmmm?"

"It's me. It's Jake."

"Oh, hi."

"You don't even sound like yourself. Your voice is so slow. Did I wake you up?"

"No, I'm just—I was just—I was resting."

"Oh . . . I stopped by this afternoon, but you weren't home."

"I was—out."

"Well, I know that now. Where were you?"

"I was—jogging."

"Around the island?"

"Uh-huh."

"So I guess that's why you're so sleepy now, huh?"

"Mmm-hmmm. Sorry."

"It's okay. I guess I'd better let you get back to sleep."

"Good night."

"Good night."


"Hello?"

"Hello?"

"Hello?"

"Hello?"

"Claire?"

"Nina? Is that you? Will you quit saying *hello* every two seconds?"

"You said it just as many times as I did."

"I did not."

"Did too!"

"Did not!"

"Did too!"

"Excuse me, but are we in the third grade?"

"No, but it sure felt like it there for a second."

"Tell me about it."

"So, listen, are we going to have some more third-grade arguments? Listen, Claire, I have a good one! Say *make me*."

"Nina—"

"Just say it. Come on, it'll be fun."

"Okay . . . make me."

*"I don't make monkeys—I just train 'em!"*

"Nina—"

"Boy, that was great. Call me anytime, and we'll do a few more."

"Wait a minute, *you* called *me*."

"I did no such thing."

"Did—"

"Hey, you were about to say *did too*."

"I wasn't."

"Were too."

"Nina, snap out of it, okay? Now, seriously, what do you want?"

"Aside from your solemn vow to join a convent and not even visit Dad and me on major holidays?"

"Okay, Nina, that's it. I'm hanging up."

"Go ahead! You're the one who called me. Hey, and where are you, anyway? Are you out with Aaron or something?"

"What are you talking about? I'm right here in the kitchen."

"You're *where?*"

"In the kitchen. How else would I have answered the phone?"

"I answered. I'm on the upstairs phone."

"You're kidding. You mean we've been arguing over the phone when we're right here in the same house?"

"Yeah, we could've been arguing in person!"

"What a waste . . . well, listen, you want some cocoa?"

"You're making cocoa? In June?"

"I felt like it."

"Oh . . . okay, I'll be down in a minute. Claire?"

"Hmmm?"

"If you're home and I'm home, who called?"

"I don't know. It must have been some short in the line or whatever."

"Or else somebody actually called us."

"And didn't say anything? Just let us talk?"

"Well, that makes more sense than the electrical short theory."

"I am not spending any more time on the phone with you, Nina. Are you coming down here or what?"

"Okay. Good-bye."

"Good-bye."

Both girls hung up. And then there was a third final soft click on the line.

Zoey sat on a sofa in a plush Washington hotel room in her new black velvet dress with a glass of champagne in her hand and tried to estimate the number of gross businessmen in Washington, D.C., who had made passes at her so far.

Okay. Let's say there were one million businessmen in D.C. And let's say that one in every four was gross. (That wasn't a very charitable estimate, but Zoey wasn't feeling very charitable.) That brought the total number of gross businessmen to 250,000, and Zoey guessed that already at least two dozen had hit on her and that meant—

Her train of thought was interrupted when the cat food salesman sitting on the couch next to her put his hand on her leg. Zoey sat up straighter and looked at his hand as though it were an alien tentacle. He hastily withdrew it.

"So, Zelda," he began.

Zoey looked at him coldly. "My name isn't Zelda," she said. "I would think you might have tried to get my name straight before you put your hand on my leg. Not that it would have made a difference." She set down her glass. "Although as a matter of fact, I'm glad you put your hand on my leg because it gives me the perfect excuse to be rude."

She stood up and walked away. Honestly. This whole stupid conference was just a big string of cocktail parties, where she and the other interns were lined up and ogled by these disgusting executive types. A cat food salesman! Wasn't she here to meet senators and politicians? And have intelligent conversation, as opposed to being chased around coffee tables? Had she left Lucas for *this*?

The mere thought of Lucas was powerful enough to make Zoey's eyes water. She thought of him this morning in the airport, hugging her from behind. Why had she left him?

A waiter walked by with another tray of champagne-filled glasses, and Zoey took one. She went onto the balcony. The hotel room was on the fiftieth floor, and the lights of the city spread out beneath her in an unreal, tiny configuration.

She took a sip of champagne and thought back to her phone call with Lucas earlier that evening. She'd told him that she loved Washington, which was true, in a way. She could have also told him that she missed Lucas and Chatham Island more than she would have thought possible. But she didn't want to burden Lucas with her loneliness when he was the one whose dad had just died and who had to get up at four every morning and work all day (as opposed to just getting dressed up and fending off cat food salesmen). No, better to let him believe that she was having a wonderful time, that it had all been worth it for her to come here.

"You look so sad," a voice next to her said.

Zoey's teeth ground together. *That cat food salesman gives all men a bad name,* she thought viciously. *He gives all cat food a bad name, all cats, practically.*

But when she looked up, she saw that it was only another intern from the conference, a guy not much older than she was. She recognized him vaguely from the youth hostel where they were staying.

She shrugged and smiled. "Maybe a little blue," she admitted.

"Homesick?" the guy asked.

Zoey considered. It wasn't home that she felt such a longing for. But what could she say? *No, I'm boy sick? Boyfriend sick? Lovesick?*

Lovesick. That's what she was. Until that moment Zoey had always thought lovesick meant heartbroken. Now . . . standing on a chilly balcony in Washington, D.C., she knew that it really meant the same as homesick, when your home was another person.

# Nina

One time Zoey was reading some book, and she said that she admired the author so much that she wanted to rip off her clothes and appear on his doorstep naked. Well, that's pretty much the difference between Zoey and me: She assumes that the guy would be delighted with this gift of her body, and I'm sure he would be. If it were me, I'd be afraid he'd call the police.

Of course, I'd show up naked on Benjamin's doorstep if I thought it might actually get his attention. I'd do it in a

heartbeat. But with my luck —
assuming Mr. Passmore didn't
answer the door and pass out in
a dead faint — Benjamin would
just say, "Excuse me," and edge
past me on his way to photography class or a film festival or
whatever. Because really, what
could possibly be interesting
about one ordinary girl (even if
she is naked) when there's the
whole rest of the world waiting to be explored?

# Five

Lucas wasn't sure he liked his relatives individually and on happy occasions, but he certainly didn't like them all at once, still hanging around after his father's funeral. The only good thing was that none of them thought he should take the boat out until tomorrow at the earliest. They wanted him to have a decent mourning period. Well, fine, he would go tomorrow.

Right now his aunt Ginger was sitting on the sofa with her arms around his mother. "Don't worry," Aunt Ginger was saying. "Lucas is a good boy. He'll stay and take care of you."

His mother blew her nose. "But for how long? He's young, he'll run off. . . ."

Lucas rustled a bag of potato chips loudly. He took out a chip and crunched it noisily. None of the relatives so much as spared him a glance.

Aunt Ginger drew his mother's head onto her shoulder. "No, no, Lucas owes it to you. . . . He'll stay and make up for the years of pain he caused you when he got sent to prison."

*Youth Authority,* Lucas corrected her silently.

"Wasn't he pardoned or paroled or something?" his uncle Joe asked.

*Good old Joe,* Lucas thought.

"A technicality," Aunt Ginger said dismissively.

"But did he do it or not?" persisted Uncle Joe.

"Of course he did it," Aunt Ginger said. "They don't send innocent people to prison, now, do they?"

The phone rang, and Lucas leaped on it as though it were the last drop of water in the desert. "Hello?" he said. "Hello? Hello? Hello?"

"Take it easy," Nina's voice answered. "I'm not calling to tell you that you won the lottery or anything."

"You don't know," Lucas muttered darkly.

"What I *am* calling about," Nina said, and paused. "Well, I don't know if you're busy or—"

"I have never been less busy in my entire life," Lucas said.

"Well, the thing is . . ." He heard Nina take a deep breath. She continued in a rush. "I owe my dad a hundred and fifty dollars, and I'm having a garage sale to raise the money. Want to come over?"

Lucas barely said good-bye to her, he was so busy rushing out the door.


Nina was standing in the Geigers' junk-filled yard, wearing a clingy black T-shirt and baggy overalls. The sun was sparkling on her brandy-colored hair.

Lucas came closer and saw that Nina was operating an ancient-looking cash register.

"Hi, Neen," he said.

She ignored him, intent on folding an infant sweater. Her unlit Lucky Strike was tucked behind her ear. "That'll be two dollars," she said in a cool, professional voice to the woman buying the sweater.

Lucas looked at the woman and hid a smile. It was Mrs. Hendricks, who'd known Nina all her life, and here Nina was pretending they'd never met.

Nina pounded viciously at a button on the cash register until the cash drawer swung reluctantly open. She made change for Mrs. Hendricks, giving her a bright smile.

"Hello, Lucas," Mrs. Hendricks said.

"Hello, Mrs. H."

"Sorry to hear about your father."

"Thank you, ma'am."

"Have a good day and come again," Nina interrupted.

Mrs. Hendricks took her infant sweater and left.

Lucas sat down on a lawn chair. "How's business?"

Nina threw herself into the chair next to him. She was bubbly and full of energy. "Business is great! I've already made a hundred dollars! From this point on it's just icing on the cake, practically."

"You've really made a hundred dollars?"

"Isn't that great?" She beamed. "Maybe I should have gotten a sales job this summer after all." She looked fondly at the cash register. "Did you see what a whiz I am at making change?"

"Oh, yes," Lucas said solemnly. "Where did you find that thing? In the attic?"

"Uh-huh." Nina tugged on one of her silver earrings. The earring was longer than her hair. It brushed her shoulder. "I was a little rusty at first, but I made Janelle come out and pretend to buy some stuff, and I caught on right away."

"So what have you sold so far?"

"Oh, this and that . . . ," she said vaguely.

"Lots of baby clothes like that sweater you just sold?"

"Oh, that wasn't a baby sweater," Nina said in a low voice. She cast a look over her shoulder at the house and apparently decided the coast was clear. "That was

36

a sweater of Claire's that I borrowed without permission, and I was planning to wash it and smuggle it back into her room, but I used the wrong temperature water or something and it shrank."

"What will happen when Claire finds out it's missing?"

"Are you kidding?" Nina looked indignant. "She has so many clothes, she'll never notice." Suddenly she giggled. "Of course, she might spot it on Mrs. Hendricks's granddaughter and think it looks familiar."

Lucas laughed. "Hey, where's Benjamin?"

"Busy," Nina said. Her voice was so clipped that Lucas lapsed into silence. They both gazed uncomfortably at the empty street. Nina sighed. "I'll get a big rush of customers when the next ferry comes in," she said. She smiled faintly. "I sure know how to show a guy a good time, don't I?"

Lucas returned the smile. "I'm fine," he said. "I was so happy when you called. If you'd said you were cleaning the oven, I still would have come over."

Nina didn't smile. "What's wrong at home?"

"Besides all the relatives hanging around and saying painfully pointed things about the kind of son I am?"

"Oh, yes, the relatives," Nina said softly. Her eyes had a faraway look. "I remember that from—from when my mom died."

Lucas was stricken. How could he have been such an idiot? Maybe it was okay to talk about what a drag funerals were, but what must it sound like to Nina? She knew, after all, what a funeral was like when it was for the person you loved most in the world.

He cleared his throat and tried to think of something to say. Should he change the subject? Was Nina going to start crying?

He glanced over at her, but she didn't seem upset, just thoughtful.

"What was your mother like?" Lucas asked softly.

A tiny frown appeared between Nina's eyebrows. "I can't always remember," she said. "I mean, most of the time I *do* remember, but it's only isolated things, like how when I was really small, she used to give me baths in the kitchen sink so she could use that sprayer thing?" Nina was tugging so hard at her earring that Lucas feared she would rip it out of her earlobe. "But I don't know what kind of *person* she was. From what people say, I guess she was Claire, only nice."

"Then in what way was she like Claire?" Lucas teased gently.

Nina laughed and let go of her earring. "Good point. Obviously she must have only *looked* like Claire." She turned serious. "Do you think that's awful, though? That I can only remember the way she used to kiss the top of my head? And not what she thought about politics or the world or whatever?"

She looked so distressed that Lucas was tempted to reach out to her. But he only said carefully, "No, I don't think it's awful. Last night I was trying to remember my father, and all I could do was picture this time he stood up too suddenly and his chair fell over and banged his ankle."

"Why did you picture that?"

"I don't know," Lucas said, "but once I saw it, I couldn't *un*see it. I tried to conjure up some other memory of my dad for, like, an hour, and I couldn't."

Nina looked at him. "This is going to sound terrible, but that makes me feel better."

Lucas smiled. "Nina, would you like to go out on my dad's boat with me one day this week?"

Her face lit up. "Oh, I'd love to—hey, look, here's my dad. He must've come home for lunch."

Mr. Geiger walked up the drive, carrying his briefcase. "Hello, Lucas," he said, and turned to Nina. "How's my little entrepreneur?"

Nina slammed the cash register a few times and presented Mr. Geiger with a big roll of bills. "Here's a hundred," she said. "If I stay out here this afternoon, I'm sure I'll have the other fifty."

Mr. Geiger looked startled. "Nina, that's excellent," he said. "I didn't think you had ten dollars' worth of stuff. What did you sell?"

Nina began ticking them off on her fingers. "I sold Claire's old prom dress for five bucks. I sold my broken hair dryer to Mrs. Kaiser's five-year-old so she can play beauty parlor. I sold, uh, a sweater." She frowned, trying to remember. "Oh, yeah, and I sold those old snow tires to Mr. Norton for forty dollars."

Lucas was studying Mr. Geiger's face. He looked like a man who was having a suspicion too horrible to put into words. Mr. Geiger's mouth worked silently for a moment, but then he did put it into words. "What snow tires?" he said in a voice like a zombie's.

"The ones that were leaning against the wall of the garage," Nina said perkily. "Why?"

Mr. Geiger set his briefcase down as though it were very heavy. "Why?" he repeated. "Because those were brand-new snow tires I bought last week for two hundred dollars."

Nina clapped a hand over her mouth. "You're kidding!"

"I wouldn't kid about this, I assure you," Mr. Geiger said. He looked at Nina, and the cigarette behind her ear, and the cash register, and his eyes were amused, despite his frown.

Lucas wondered what it would be like to have a father who loved you as much as that.

# Six

You could see into the Passmores' kitchen from the Cabrals' house, and from a small hill nearby you could see into the Cabrals' house. And if you climbed partway up an old oak tree, the way Jake did, you could see right into Kate's room.

Jake wasn't proud of spying on Kate, but he felt he had to do it. He didn't know what was wrong with her, but he knew something was. Jake was an alcoholic, and so he knew better than a lot of people when someone was lying—because he had done it so many times himself. And Kate had done it last night. Twice.

*I was—out. . . . I was—jogging. . . .*

It was the hesitation that gave her away. It was a very small hesitation, maybe only half a second, but it told Jake several things. First of all, it told him that she had not been out, nor had she been jogging. Otherwise she wouldn't have hesitated. If you had the flu and someone asked you about it, you said, *I have the flu.* Unless you really had a hangover, and then you said, *I have—the flu.* You needed that half second to give your frantic brain time to supply you with a plausible lie. (Sometimes your brain was better at this than at other times.)

Anyway, those two hesitations in their phone conversation had made up Jake's mind. Kate had a secret. He didn't think it was drinking, but it could be. He knew better than to rule that out with anyone. It could be family trouble, it could be another guy, it could be any number of things. But Jake was sitting here in an oak tree—armed with binoculars, two peanut butter sandwiches, and three sodas—and he was going to find out what it was.

It wasn't exactly the world's most interesting stake-out. Jake got there at eleven in the morning, and he didn't see hide nor hair of Kate until nearly one, when he spotted her tousled red head moving around in her bedroom.

Then the blue-gas light from a television filled the window and stayed that way for an hour and a half. Jake couldn't see Kate, but he assumed she was out of sight on the bed.

Finally the television was turned off, and Kate drifted back into his view. She still had bed-head and was wearing a pair of blue-striped pajamas. He could see her as she sat down at her computer. She turned it on and began working. Well, Jake assumed she was working until he put the binoculars to his eyes and saw that she was playing computer solitaire. Kate playing solitaire! And not just one game, but dozens. Jake's mind went numb just from thinking about it, and he was overjoyed forty-five minutes later when Kate turned off the computer and stretched.

She walked out of sight, and a few seconds later the light in her bedroom flipped off. Jake scrambled out of the tree and slid around the front of the house just in time to see her turn the corner.

He followed her first to Passmores' and waited outside. What was she getting?

"Jake?"

He spun around, heart hammering. Christopher stood in the street. "Oh, hi, Chris," he said, trying not to sound impatient. If Kate came out now, she'd just avoid him and go back home.

Luckily Christopher seemed pretty preoccupied himself. "Have you seen Aisha or Kendra?" he said, snapping his fingers like he was in a big hurry.

"No, sorry," Jake said. *How would I?* he thought. *I've been sitting like a bird in a tree for hours.*

"I've got to find them," Christopher murmured, and went off down the street. Jake sighed with relief and stepped into a doorway just as Kate emerged from Passmores'. She was carrying a white paper bag, spotted with grease. Even from fifty feet Jake could recognize the smell of ribs. He frowned. Kate almost always ate healthy, nutritious things. If she had barbecue, it would be one or two ribs, a splurge, not a whole bag.

He began trailing her again. She seemed to be heading toward home, and he closed the distance between them. Who cared if she saw him now? He had just as much reason to be on the street as she did. From close-up he could see that she hadn't bothered to take off her blue-striped pajama top—she'd merely tucked it into a pair of loose white shorts. Her hair looked different, too. It looked—kind of dirty.

Kate stopped suddenly in front of the mailbox and dug in the pocket of her white shorts. She pulled out an envelope and opened the flap of the mailbox. She hesitated. She took the letter back out and looked at it. She flipped it over. What was she checking for? Jake could see it was sealed. She opened the mailbox again. Put her hand in, but withdrew it still holding the letter. She did that once more.

Jake's eyebrows drew together. She was acting peculiarly.

Kate set the white paper bag on the sidewalk. *Gross,* Jake thought. Those bags weren't that thick, and the sidewalk was filthy. He began walking. She was opening the letter.

"Kate, what are you doing?"

She looked up, startled. "Hi, Jake." She passed a hand over her unwashed hair. "How are you?"

He ignored her and reached for the letter. "What is that?" he said quietly. "And why are you so afraid to mail it?"

She smiled. It was a horrible smile: false, bright, meant to mislead him. "It's just a Visa bill," she said, showing him the envelope.

"And why have you taken it in and out of the mailbox a hundred times?"

For a moment the fake smile faltered. "I was worried—I suddenly thought that maybe I hadn't put the check in the envelope," she said. "Or not the right check—or something."

He took the envelope from her gently. She let him. He looked inside. The check was there, along with the payment stub. He glanced at it. "Kate, this bill is ninety days overdue."

She was silent for a moment. "I know," she said. The bright smile was gone. Instead she looked horribly confused. "It happens every month," she said miserably. "I go to mail it, and then I get all nervous and I open it, and then I have to redo the envelope and it doesn't get done, and . . . I don't know. It just keeps happening."

Jake heard none of the telltale hesitations in her voice. He didn't know what she was talking about, but he knew she was telling the truth. He stepped closer to her and put his arm around her. He traced the curve of her face gently. "Tell me what's wrong," he said. "Just tell me, and I'll help you fix it."

43

Kate's arms went around his neck in a suffocating grip. "I don't think you can," she said, so softly he could barely hear her.

Benjamin was lying on his bed in front of his television, watching the sex scenes of various movies. (He was fast-forwarding through the other, unsexy parts.) Right now he was watching the ice cube scene from *9½ Weeks,* which Christopher had recommended, saying that it was "an oldie but a goodie." Well, privately Benjamin felt that all the sex scenes of all the movies were goodies, oldie or otherwise. Imagine losing your sight thinking that every girl, except maybe your mother, was "yucky," and regaining your sight to find that every girl, except maybe your mother, was fantastically appealing? Benjamin had had girlfriends when he was blind, but now that he could see, he sometimes looked around him—on the ferry, in the grocery store, in the park—and thought he would lose his mind over how beautiful the girls looked.

Eventually, however, watching sex scenes in his darkened bedroom on a beautiful summer day began to seem a little too seedy, even for him, so he turned off the TV and went outside. The sunshine was so bright, it hurt his eyes. But then, almost everything hurt his eyes, either because it was bright or because it was beautiful or because he had missed seeing it so much. That made him think of Nina, and he wondered where she was and what she was doing.

Then, as if his thinking about her had caused her to appear, Nina strolled out of the Passmores' garage, wearing army shorts and a yellow tank top. She had a tree trimmer in her hands.

Benjamin smiled. Movie or no movie, Nina was still the most beautiful girl he knew. "Hey, Nina," he called. "What are you doing sneaking out of our garage?"

She looked over at him standing on the porch, and a smile of genuine pleasure lit her face. "Benjamin," she said delightedly. "I'm so happy to see you."

Her words were innocent enough, but they made Benjamin feel terribly guilty. Of course she was happy to see him—she hardly ever did anymore.

"I'm happy to see you, too," he said, making his voice casual. "What are you up to?"

Nina wrinkled her nose. "Now I owe my dad an extra two hundred dollars for his snow tires, and he's letting me work some of it off by trimming the trees."

Benjamin laughed. "How much is he paying you?"

"Don't ask." Nina rolled her eyes. "Let's just say we barely have enough trees and shrubs to make it worth my while. Plus, he couldn't find our tree trimmer and accused me of selling *that* in the garage sale, too."

"Did you?"

"No, it turns out we never had one; the gardener always brought his own. But I called your dad at the restaurant, and he said I could borrow yours." She shifted awkwardly, readjusting the strap of the tree trimmer on her shoulder. "That's my oh-so-exciting life. What are you doing?"

"I don't know," Benjamin said. "I might catch the ferry over to the mainland or hang out here."

Nina's face brightened. "Well, why don't you come hang out with me?" she said. "It won't be dangerous, I promise. At least not for you. You can lie in the hammock while I risk life and limb for five dollars a tree—"

"Five dollars a tree? Nina, that's peanuts!"

"I told you it was barely worth my while, didn't I? Anyway, do you want to come? I might need you there to call the fire department if I get stuck in the tree."

"The fire department?" Benjamin was confused.

"Yes, well, that's who they always call on TV when

cats climb up in trees and can't get down. I figure it's the same with girls." She paused. "So . . . what do you say?"

Benjamin hesitated. He knew that if he went over and watched Nina trim trees, it would be fun. Nina would make him laugh, and Janelle would serve him ice-cold lemonade, and he could lie in the hammock and spend a lazy afternoon that way. But part of him chafed at the idea. Hadn't he spent long enough— *years* long enough—lying around while other people did things? Wasn't that exactly the kind of thing he would have done when he was blind? Of course, he'd already spent the morning lying around watching parts of movies, so what difference—

But suddenly he realized that he had hesitated far too long. Nina's face had a closed, hurt look.

"Never mind," she said suddenly. "I'm sure you'll find something else to do."

"Nina . . . ," he began.

"It's okay," she said. "Call me later—if you *want* to."

She walked off down the street, her slim shoulders bent slightly under the weight of the tree trimmer. Benjamin watched her go and his heart went out to her, but he stayed where he was.

# Seven

Aaron was happy when he saw Claire standing at the mailbox. It meant he wouldn't have to go inside and risk seeing his mother or Burke.

He walked down the street toward her. She was wearing jeans and a white blouse with ruffles and lace and a drawstring neckline. Aaron supposed that blouse would look dumb on most girls, but not on Claire. Her dark hair was full and luxurious, and her dark lashes cast black crescents on her pale cheeks. Aaron guessed that most girls who saw Claire in that romantic blouse went out and bought themselves one.

He whistled, and she looked up and smiled slightly. She folded an envelope in half quickly and slipped it into her pocket. Aaron leaned an elbow against the mailbox and looked at her.

She tucked a strand of hair behind her ear. "Hello."

"Hello, yourself."

"Is there any particular reason you have a blanket tucked under your arm?"

He shifted. "I thought maybe I could interest you in exploring a deserted part of the island with me."

She raised an eyebrow. "We could do that without a blanket."

"True." Aaron pretended to look thoughtful. "But what if we get tired and want to lie down?"

Her full lips twisted. "My, but you think of everything. What were you going to tell the Midget if she saw you?"

"That my room was cold at night and I needed an extra blanket."

"In June?"

Aaron gave up trying to stand so far away from her. He lifted the thick dark hair and kissed the side of her neck. "I'm extremely warm-blooded," he said.

She shivered a little bit. "I can see that."

"So do you want to go—exploring?"

She linked her arm through his. "Sure."

They walked back up the street. "Are you going to tell me what that envelope was that you hid in your pocket?"

"A letter from my other boyfriend."

"The one you went on the blind date with?"

"Hardly," Claire said. "I'm not sure he could write his own name, let alone a letter."

"Good."

"Why?"

Aaron stopped and put his arms around her. "Because I'm the possessive type," he said. He kissed her.

She put her hands against his chest. "Aaron, your mom is going to see us. Or someone else will and tell her."

"I don't care." He kissed her again. "I'll promise to make my bed every morning for a year."

Claire laughed. "Nina's already making everyone's bed. For twenty-five cents a day."

Aaron realized suddenly that he could count the number of times he'd heard Claire laugh on the fingers on one hand. And that was too bad because she had a great laugh: low, resonant, and silvery.

He buried his face in her neck. At that moment he loved her completely.

Dear Nina,

Today we were all supposed to go on this bus tour of D.C., but about two blocks into it the bus crunched over a VW and we all had to stand around in this hellishly humid weather while the police sorted everything out. Anyway, the tour was supposed to last all day, but we came back early (obviously) and now I'm in my room, writing to you.

All the interns are staying at this youth hostel. It's okay, although the bathroom is down the hall and you have to take your shampoo in a bucket. My roommate is this girl named Mary Beth, and the less said about her, the better. Also, if you thought the food was bad in high school, you should eat here. Last night this Swedish guy had to have his stomach pumped.

Later they told us it was a barbiturate overdose, but I'm sure it was really the tuna casserole.

MaryBeth left her purse on the bus (which is now being towed off to the bus headquarters or whatever), and she's going to be off all afternoon trying to get it back.

I haven't told Lucas yet but I think I might be asked to stay here a few extra days. We had to write essays about our hometowns (original topic, huh?) when we first got here, and based on the essays, they're choosing one person to stay on and do a week-long internship at the <u>Washington Post.</u> Some of our group leaders seem pretty intrigued with the island concept.

But even if I did get chosen

50

I probably wouldn't stay. I miss you all too much.

Love, Zoey

P.S. I hope you're being nice to Lucas.

Dear Aisha,

I'm mainly writing to remind you of the time that Nina had a crush on the camp counselor and she wrote him and signed her letter "Your friend, Nina," and he wrote back and signed his letter, "Just friends, Rob." She gets furious whenever I bring that up, but I always think it's hilarious.

All the interns are staying at this youth hostel. It's okay, although the bathroom is down the hall and you have to take your shampoo in a bucket. My roommate is this girl named MaryBeth, and practically every piece of clothing she owns has lambs or rosebuds embroidered on it. When I told her where I was from, she said, "An island in Maine! That's so quaint!" I wanted to say, "At least I don't dress like a Holly Hobby doll." (Remember them?)

Oops, I have to go. This girl

from Bangor and I are going
to interview the Maine senator
in best cub-reporter style. I'm
sure he's shaking in his
shoes, ha ha.

Just friends,
Zoey

P.S. Don't you hate people
who write "ha ha" after their
own jokes?

Dear Benjamin,

Remember how before I left, Mom told me about a hundred times to be sure to call her old college roommate's son? Well, of course I never did, but I met him by accident when our bus ran his car over. (It's a long story.) Anyway, I was totally thrilled by this coincidence and told everyone on the bus, plus two policemen, but they couldn't have cared less. Actually no one (but Mom) will probably care very much, either, but sometimes you like random family-accident stories, so I'm telling you.

I'm also enclosing two post-cards. The one of that run-down building that looks like a prison is the youth hostel where I live. The other one is a hotel where I was proposi-tioned by a cat food salesman (another long story).

I hope you and Nina are paying lots of attention to

Lucas. Do you think it would be terrible for Lucas if I stayed on here an extra few days or so?

Love,

Zoey

Dear Lucas,

I'm not even keeping a journal of this trip because I don't think I would ever want to read it. Forty years from now I would say to myself, I wonder what I was doing that June? and I'd open my journal and there would be thirty straight pages of extremely small letters reading "I miss Lucas" over and over.

Because I do miss you, Lucas. I wish I'd never left. I don't know how we're going to manage in the fall, but right now we just have to concentrate on the fact that we will be together in two weeks at the latest, and then for the rest of the summer. Yes, we will! Yes, we will!

All my love,
Zoey

# Eight

Lara's first thought when she saw Mr. Passmore in the 7-Eleven in Weymouth was: *What the hell is he doing here?* Followed quickly by: *Thank God I don't have beer in my hands.*

Of course, that was just a matter of luck. If Mr. Passmore had come in thirty seconds later, Lara would have had a couple of six-packs in her hands. But luck was with her today. She just happened to be standing there, innocently holding a frozen burrito.

"Lara," Mr. Passmore said. His expression was almost comically divided: half pleasure at seeing her, half fearful that she would misbehave.

Lara didn't know whether to call him "Dad" or "Mr. Passmore" or what. Finally she just gave him a big, sugary smile and said, "What brings you out here?"

"There's a warehouse nearby where I usually go to pick up some things for the restaurant," Mr. Passmore said.

*Rats,* Lara thought. She'd chosen this 7-Eleven because it was so far out of the way.

"What are you doing over here?" Mr. Passmore asked.

Lara was caught completely off guard. Good Lord, she should have been thinking about her own cover story instead of wondering about what Mr. Passmore was doing here. How could she have been so stupid?

She was so nervous, she dropped the frozen burrito. She and Mr. Passmore leaned over for it at the same time, and their hands touched briefly as he gave it to her. "It's okay, Lara," he said softly. "I know."

She swallowed, and there was an audible click in her throat. "You do?"

He looked puzzled. "At least I think I do. Isn't there an A.A. meeting over in that old church across the street?"

The rush of relief through Lara's veins was nearly as sweet and refreshing as—well, as a nice cold beer.

"Yes," she said. "You're exactly right."

It wasn't as though it was such an awfully big lie. She did go to A.A. She just hadn't gone to the one Mr. Passmore was thinking of. But she was making progress, she thought. She only allowed herself to get drunk on Thursday nights, and only on beer.

She and Mr. Passmore got in line. He was buying a Slurpee, Lara saw without surprise. Cherry Coke mixture. Lara would have thought someone like herself, who could stand the taste of peppermint schnapps straight, would have to look pretty hard to find a drink that turned her stomach. But evidently not.

"So, I've missed seeing you around," Mr. Passmore said shyly.

Lara smiled at him. "Really?" she said, but her mind was almost completely absorbed by two thoughts that had nothing to do with missing Mr. Passmore.

The first thought was a sincere hope that the clerk wouldn't recognize her and say, *What, no beer for you today?*

The second was the realization that she had an opportunity to score almost limitless brownie points.

The line moved forward until Lara and Mr. Passmore were next to the cash register. The clerk looked up, and Lara held her breath. But he just looked bored. Luck really was with her today.

Mr. Passmore put his Slurpee on the counter, along with a bag of potato chips. Lara set her frozen burrito on the counter, too. "This is all together," she told the clerk.

Mr. Passmore smiled. "Well, thank you very much, Lara," he said.

Lara tried not to roll her eyes. Ponytail or not, he was sure a sap.

"You're welcome," she said lightly. She took a roll of bills out of her pocket and paid the clerk, but she didn't put the money back in her pocket. "Here," she said awkwardly, holding the money out to Mr. Passmore. "It's only fifty dollars, but—"

"Lara, I can't take your money," Mr. Passmore said.

"Why not? I owe it to you." Lara leaned over and slipped the money into Mr. Passmore's shirt pocket. "It's the least I can do. I owe you lots more than that."

"But Lara, you work so hard for your money," Mr. Passmore said. He took the money right back out. "I hate to see—"

"You work hard for your money, too," she said, gently but firmly. "And I wasn't thinking of that when I broke your window—well, I just wasn't thinking, period."

"But surely you must need—"

"Oh, I'm working a lot of hours, even saving a little," Lara said dismissively. She was gratified to see a glimmer of respect in his eyes. Lara bet Zoey never did anything but spend money. Naturally Mr. Passmore would love a daughter who wasn't milking him dry. He didn't need to know that Lara had gotten the fifty dollars two hours earlier when she returned a blouse she'd bought on sale and they rang it up wrong and gave her back full price.

"Go on," she urged softly. "Keep it."

Mr. Passmore smiled at her. "Okay," he said. The money went back into his pocket. "On the condition that you let me cook you dinner one night this week."

"It's a deal."

"Tomorrow?"

"Sounds good," Lara said.

"Okay, we'll see you at seven." He took a few steps toward his van, then turned back to her. "I'm amazed by the change in you, Lara," he said. "It's unbelievable."

She smiled and shrugged a little. *That's the word for it,* she thought.

Aisha watched Kendra as she bent over and tucked a sheet under a mattress, making a careful hospital corner. Even in jeans and an old T-shirt Kendra's figure was clearly outlined. Aisha thought, not for the first time, how happy she was that Kendra really was Christopher's sister. She would be too threatened by that body and those cheekbones to accept her as one of Christopher's long-lost "friends."

"Whew," Kendra said, straightening up. Aisha saw that the famous cheekbones were flushed, and tiny diamonds of moisture dotted Kendra's upper lip. It only made her look more glamorous, like an actress playing a chambermaid, as opposed to Aisha, who just looked like a hot, sweaty girl.

She smiled at Kendra. "How's your back holding up?"

Kendra stretched. "Not too bad, considering."

"Considering what?"

"Considering I've made more beds today than, like, all the other days of my life put together."

"We can take a break if you like," Aisha said. "It's almost lunchtime, anyway." She was pleased with Kendra and with herself for thinking to give her a job. Kendra was a quick learner, and even if she wasn't the world's most energetic worker, she hadn't had to be told more than once how to arrange the hand towels or how to position the soaps or how to turn back the sheets or any of the other million things that Aisha's mother insisted on.

Almost as soon as she thought of her mother, Mrs. Gray poked her head through the door. She looked around the room, her sharp eyes missing nothing. "You girls have done a lovely job in every room," she said approvingly. "Why don't you take a break and go to the park for lunch? I've already wrapped up some sandwiches for you."

Aisha smiled at her mother gratefully. "That would be great, Mom," she said.

She and Kendra went down to the kitchen, picked up their sandwiches, and headed over to the ferry landing. The summer breeze felt wonderful after a morning in the B&B, where all the fancy window dressings made Aisha feel claustrophobic.

Once they were settled and eating, Aisha asked casually, "Any more stories about Christopher for me?" She had been dying to ask all morning, but she wanted Kendra to feel that she liked her for her own self, not just as some sort of human encyclopedia of Christopher facts.

Kendra looked more interested in peering under the bread of her sandwich. "What do you want to know?"

"Well . . . was he a good brother? What was that like?"

Kendra apparently found the sandwich to her liking because she stopped poking it with her finger and began eating. She looked thoughtful. "He was a great older brother," she said. "My mom tells this story about how when I was born, he insisted on keeping my box in his room and—"

Aisha looked puzzled. "Box?"

Kendra gestured with her hand because her mouth was full. She swallowed and said, "Yeah, you know, the box I slept in."

"You mean a crib?"

"No, I mean a box. Like, um, oranges or whatever come in."

"You mean a cardboard box?" Aisha tried to keep her voice from sounding so shocked, but it was hard. Imagine having a baby and keeping her in a cardboard box. Of course, Ms. Passmore had told her and Christopher once that when Benjamin was born, they had had to make a bed for him out of one of their dresser drawers. But that seemed romantic and rustic. A cardboard box just sounded—sordid.

Luckily Kendra didn't seem to notice her tone. "And he used to walk me to and from school every single day until I was about fifteen," she said. "I guess he figured I'd be safe."

Aisha didn't ask safe from what. She had a feeling that walking to school in Christopher and Kendra's neighborhood probably held more dangers than just crossing the street.

Kendra finished her sandwich and lay back on the grass. "Speaking of Christopher," she said, "maybe he'll lay off me now that I'm making a little money."

Aisha smiled. "You did a good job," she said. "I'm sure my parents would love to have you work a couple days a week."

Kendra rolled her eyes. "But Christopher will probably want me to work about ten jobs a week like he does. He never lets up on me."

Aisha hesitated. "He does seem awfully—curt sometimes," she said.

Kendra sighed. "He has his reasons, I guess."

"But what possible reason could he have?" Aisha said. She laid her hand on Kendra's arm. "You're his *family*."

Kendra looked uncomfortable. "I think that's the problem, actually," she said. "I know things, and he's afraid—"

"Kendra! Aisha!"

They looked up. Christopher was standing above them. His voice was cheerful, but Aisha thought his face looked tight and nervous. "Mind if I join you?"

"Of course not," she said. He sat down, and she leaned over to kiss him. His lips were dry as cotton. She studied his face, but he looked away.

"So what are you two talking about?" he asked.

"Girl stuff," Kendra said promptly.

Christopher cleared his throat. He picked up a crust of sandwich and ate it. Aisha was still looking at him. The breeze from the ocean had picked up, and their picnic spot was cool.

But Christopher was sweating.

# Nine

The phone rang in the Geigers' brightly lit kitchen for the fifth time that evening and Claire snatched it off the hook, but she didn't say hello. She merely held the receiver to her ear, listening. Yes, there it was, the faint but unmistakable sound of breathing, just like in the other calls.

*Well, buddy,* Claire thought. *Two can play at this game.* She made the sound of her own inhaling and exhaling louder. Maybe this would confuse him— her?—they?—enough so that—

"Claire, you know Dad doesn't like you calling Chippendale's nine hundred number all the time," Nina said from behind her.

Claire dropped the phone back onto the cradle hastily.

Nina crossed the kitchen and began measuring coffee into the coffeemaker. "So I'm guessing that was the crank caller?" she asked.

Claire's jaw dropped before she could stop it. "How did you know about that?" she asked.

"How do you think?" Nina said. "Same way as you. I pick up the phone and he *breathes* at me."

Claire didn't like the sound of that. If Nina was

intercepting calls, too, that meant they were even more frequent than she thought.

Nina leaned against the sink, looking thoughtful. "I wish he were the kind of nut who at least *said* something," she mused. "I mean, why not use a little imagination while you're at it?"

"Maybe he's just getting started," Claire said. She had regained her composure.

Nina's coffee began to percolate, and she poured some into a glass with ice. "Did I ever tell you about the obscene call we got when I was, like, ten years old?" she asked. "I answered the phone and some man said, 'Who's this?' and I said, 'Nina,' because I didn't know any better, and we began talking back and forth about school and stuff, and then the man said, 'Nina, I have something hot and heavy in my hand; what do you think it is?' and I said, 'Um, a potato?' because I didn't know what else he could be talking about and—"

"Thanks for that stroll down memory lane," Claire said wryly. "I'll be sure to ask if it's the same guy—"

"Sandy," Nina said. "His name was Sandy, which I remember because even at the age of ten I didn't think there was a *less* scary name than Sandy."

"Well, next time Sandy calls me, I'll be sure to tell him that—"

"Wait a minute," Nina said. "Why are you so sure he's calling *you?*"

Claire frowned. "I didn't say that."

"Yes, you did. You said, next time he calls *me*. Listen, he may be calling *Dad,* for all we know. Your ego is incredible." She flounced out of the kitchen, splashing a little of her iced coffee as she went.

Claire sighed and sat down at the kitchen table. She wished that Nina was right, that maybe the calls were meant for whoever answered the phone. But she knew better. She reached into her pocket and took out two envelopes with her name printed in block letters. One had been in the mailbox yesterday, one today.

Claire studied the envelopes. One had a Portland postmark, but that could mean anything or nothing. The other worried her because it had no postmark. Which meant that someone had actually walked right up to their mailbox, had actually been right on the Geigers' property, in order to deliver it. She didn't like that at all.

She opened both envelopes and shook a snapshot out of each one and put them on the kitchen table. Then she lined them up, touching the edges with her fingertips, and examined them.

They were clearly both photographs of the same thing, but—what? Like the first photo she had received, she could only make out a glowing, hazy brightness. In the most recent picture she thought she could detect a shape, a rectangle. Well, great, so it was a glowing, hazy rectangle. What did that tell her?

She flipped the snapshots over. On the back of today's someone had written, *I'm getting closer.*

Claire's hand shook as she replaced the photographs in the envelopes. Sandy might not have succeeded in scaring Nina when she was ten, but whoever *this* was, he was scaring Claire now. Badly.

# Claire

10:55 p.m. Seventy-nine degrees. Overcast, with winds from the south-west.

So earlier today I did something really dumb. I went into Nina's room and looked at one of those damn true-crime novels she reads all the time. It was one about a serial killer. Why is it that serial killers always kill young women? Well, that's neither here nor there, I guess.

Anyway, in the middle of the book there was a photograph section, and one of them really bothered me. It was a picture of one of the victims. She's smiling into the camera in this really friendly way, like she's

probably a nice person, but there's
also something a little bit fearful in
her eyes. Like even back when the
picture was taken, she knew what was
going to happen to her. . . .

# Ten

At first Lucas thought that Nina wasn't there at the marina to meet him. Well, he could hardly blame her. *He* didn't want to be here, either. Who in their right mind would want to get up at four in the morning to handle freezing wet ropes and stinking lobsters all day long?

It was then that he saw the drunk asleep on the marina deck. At least he thought it was a drunk. Who else would be passed out on the cold wet deck, wearing a ragged flannel shirt and snoring softly? He looked closer. It was Nina.

He shook her gently. "Hey," he said. "Good morning."

Nina groaned and sat up. "I was so afraid of over-sleeping that I came down here superearly to wait for you," she said.

Lucas crouched next to her and opened a thermos. He poured a cup of coffee and handed it to her. "This will help a little bit," he said, although the truth was that nothing helped. It was four in the morning, and nothing could make you forget it.

He screwed the top back on the thermos and led Nina onto the boat. He cast off the lines and then joined her in the cabin. She was sitting uncomfortably on the small metal bench. He grinned. "Not too luxurious, is it?" He shook out an old plaid blanket and tucked it around her.

"Now, keep me company for a little while," he said. He started the engine and began steering the boat out of its slip. "Then you can sleep while I work, and I should have some downtime this afternoon."

Nina nestled back against the wall. She yawned, and her hair looked like she hadn't brushed it, but then, it always looked a little bit that way. *Poor Nina,* Lucas thought. He knew she was only coming on the fishing boat as some sort of favor to Zoey. Maybe she'd already been chosen to stay the extra week and Zoey just hadn't told him yet. He wondered bitterly what Zoey would have to do for Nina in return. What was the payback for keeping someone's poor lonely boyfriend company? A new CD? A sweater?

"How much sleep did you get?" Lucas asked Nina.

"Actually a lot," she said. "I started reading *Moby Dick* at nine, and I was sound asleep by nine-thirty."

"Why were you reading *Moby Dick*?"

"Because I was going fishing with you," she said, as though he should understand, "and that was the only book about fishing in the house."

Lucas was touched. Most people wouldn't even *go* on the fishing boat, let alone try to research it. "Well," he said, "you're about to experience the real thing and see just how deadly it is."

Nina sipped her coffee. "It doesn't seem like such a horrible job to me," she said.

Lucas looked at her. "It doesn't?"

She shook her head, still warming her hands on the coffee cup. "No, it really doesn't. A. You work for yourself. Now, you might not fully appreciate how wonderful that is until you try to polish silverware with Janelle hovering over you, saying, *Don't leave any gunk between the tines* every two seconds."

Lucas looked puzzled. "Why are you polishing silverware?"

"It's part of my dad's Great Payment Plan."

"How's it going?"

"Uh, *slowly* would probably be the best word. I'm thinking of selling myself into white slavery and just giving my dad a lump sum."

"Do you actually know where to go to sell yourself into white slavery?"

Nina looked thoughtful. "No. Although once in Portland, I got in a taxi and the guy took off in the complete opposite direction of where I wanted to go, and it did cross my mind that he might try to sell me into slavery."

"Did he?"

"Oh, no, I was just turned around. He was actually going the right way."

The water was choppier out on the open sea. The engine was working harder now. "What's *B?*" Lucas asked suddenly.

"*B?*"

"Yes. You said it wasn't such a bad job because *A,* I'm my own boss. What's *B?*"

"Oh." She knit her eyebrows together. "Oh, yeah, I remember. *B.* You can leave everyone behind. How would you like to be Christopher and work at the Passmores', where everyone knows right where to find him when they want something?"

"Well—"

"Or what about Aisha," Nina said. "She works right in her very own house, and there's no getting away from it ever!"

"I see what you mean," Lucas said slowly. "What's *C?*"

"There is no *C*. Only *A* and *B*."

"Oh." Lucas was pretty pleased with *A* and *B*, though. Everyone else just felt sorry for him. His mother, his relatives, Zoey. Zoey especially. It seemed to him that he could sense pity rolling off her in great waves sometimes. But Nina looked at him and only saw the positives.

He glanced over at her, wrapped up in the plaid blanket. "Hey," he said, "why don't you sell *Claire* into white slavery and give your dad that money?"

Nina laughed delightedly. "That's a great idea," she said. "My dad wouldn't let me get the snow tires back from Mr. Norton because he said a deal was a deal. So if he's not a total hypocrite, we would never see Claire again."

Lucas laughed, too, which wasn't something he'd ever done on his father's fishing boat before.

"What a thoughtful son I have," Sarah Mendel said in her usual affectionate tone. "Not every son would come all the way out to the island just to have breakfast with his mother."

Aaron wasn't surprised that she overlooked the fact that he hadn't called first. A truly considerate son would have called and arranged to have breakfast with his mother, as opposed to showing up unannounced and having his mother fix him breakfast while she had a cup of coffee and kept him company. But his mother always overlooked anything that didn't mesh perfectly with her image of Aaron.

He leaned against the counter while she got out the pots and pans. "Mom, you don't have to make such a big production," he said.

"Don't be silly," she said. "I like to cook for you. Now, what would you like? Pretend I'm a short-order cook."

He smiled down into her trusting face, as open and simple as a daisy. "Okay. I'd like two eggs over easy, a side order of bacon, unbuttered toast with jam on the side, and hash browns. And when I say hash browns, I mean hash *browns;* I don't like hash whites."

His mother laughed delightedly. That was the way she always ordered hash browns. "Coming right up," she said, getting a potato out of the fridge and the grater out of a cupboard.

"So where is everyone?" Aaron asked.

"Well, Burke's at work, of course," his mother said. "And Nina got a call from Benjamin and went jackrabbiting over there."

Aaron waited for her to say where Claire was, but she didn't. He withheld an impatient sigh. It was Claire he had come to see in the first place. "And Claire?" he said finally, keeping his voice light.

"Oh, she went off to the mainland," his mother said. "She said she wouldn't be back until late afternoon."

Aaron was disappointed. He wanted to see Claire; he missed her. Maybe he should call Mia. She might be free and—

*No,* he told himself sternly. He liked Mia, but he loved Claire. He had to keep that idea firmly in mind.

"So has the band gotten any new gigs?" his mother asked him.

Aaron wondered why it was always so hilarious when parents used slang. Furthermore, why didn't they *know* it was hilarious? Why didn't his mother say *show* or something instead of *gig?*

"Yeah, actually we have a show the day after tomorrow in Weymouth at a bar called the Sand Bar," he said. "The other guys are coming up from Connecticut tonight."

"Oh, honey, that's great," his mother said. Then she

gasped. "Oh, no, I've broken the yolk in one of your eggs. Will you get me a fresh one out of the fridge?"

"Mom, I can eat an egg with a broken yolk, for heaven's sake."

"Aaron, please. I just like things to be nice."

He sighed. He knew that was true. "Here, Ma." He handed her the egg. "I'll be back in a sec. I want to wash my hands."

Aaron walked off casually toward the bathroom, but then he detoured abruptly and slipped up the two flights of stairs to Claire's room. Her desktop was immaculate as always, but he found a pencil and a piece of paper in a drawer. He chewed on the end of the pencil for a second and then wrote rapidly:

*Hey, how would you like to come to the Sand Bar on Friday and stand around looking gorgeous and distracting me and every other guy in the place? I'll call you tonight. I love you. A.*

He got back to the kitchen just as his mother was setting his plate on the table. He pulled up a chair, and she sat across from him with her coffee. Aaron took a bite of his hash browns and smiled at his mother absently. His mind was still on the note. Claire would like the *I love you* part.

"What are you thinking?" his mother asked.

"That you make the best breakfasts in the world," he said automatically, and his mother's expression melted, as he had known it would. Sometimes he wished she weren't such an easy touch. Sometimes he actually admired old sharp-eyed Burke. He supposed Burke was a pretty good judge of character, probably from having to approve all those loan applications at the bank.

"What are your plans for the rest of the day, sweetie?" his mother asked.

"I don't know; hang out with you?"

"Oh, Aaron, I'd love that, but I have to show a house later." His mother looked touched.

He grinned sheepishly. "Well, I should've called first."

Sarah stood up to clear his plate. Her fingers touched his dark curls. "I hate to think of you being lonely," she said. "Why—why don't you call Mia?"

Aaron took a sip of his orange juice. The sun slanted through the window and warmed him pleasantly. He felt full and content. His mother wanted him to call Mia. He couldn't disappoint his own mother, could he?

# Eleven

"So how did it go this morning?" Christopher asked. He marveled at Aisha as she leaned against the wall near the restaurant's back entrance. It had to be well over ninety degrees in the kitchen, but Aisha looked fresh and cool. She wore a blue halter and denim shorts. Christopher was looking at her legs, which were smooth and beautifully muscled and the color of honey.

"It went really well," Aisha said, smiling. "My mom likes Kendra, and Kendra likes the work."

"Great," Christopher said, trying to sound sincere.

Silently he wondered how he could have been so stupid. He had hoped that forcing Kendra to get a job would make her so unhappy that she'd leave. Now just the opposite had happened. She was putting down roots. And she was making money, so he wouldn't even have the you-don't-contribute-to-expenses excuse.

"You don't sound like you really think it's great," Aisha said. "What's wrong, Christopher? Don't you want Kendra to be happy?"

Christopher flipped a steak on the grill. "Of course I want Kendra to be happy," he said. At least it was the truth, he told himself. He pulled the french fry basket out of the deep fryer.

"Well, good," Aisha said doubtfully. "Anyway, I like having her work there. I'm getting very close to her."

Suddenly Christopher's hand shook, and the french fry basket threw a thin rope of boiling oil across the sensitive webbing of flesh between his thumb and forefinger. "Goddamn it!" he shouted. He dropped the basket back into the oil and stuck his hand into the pie pan of ice he used for garnishes.

"Christopher!" Aisha said softly. She didn't ask him if he was all right, Christopher supposed because he was so obviously not all right. Instead she put one hand on his wrist, as if to keep his hand in the ice, and with the other hand she drew small comforting circles on his back.

In truth, Christopher barely felt the burn. All he could do was hear Aisha saying, *I'm getting very close to her. . . . I'm getting very close to her.*

She couldn't have said anything worse. He looked at her now, her lovely face next to his, so concerned, and he felt sick to his stomach. Kendra could destroy everything in the blink of an eye. And she was just irresponsible enough to do it.

"Keep your hand in the ice," Aisha said. "I'm going to go get Mr. Passmore."

"I'm right here," Mr. Passmore said from the doorway. "What happened?"

"Just an oil burn," Christopher said tightly.

Mr. Passmore looked worried. "Do you need to go to the emergency room?"

Christopher drew his hand out of the ice. The oil had left a raised pink welt that would doubtless blister, but it didn't look serious, just painful. "No, I don't think so."

"Well, go on home at any rate," Mr. Passmore said. "There's only one customer, and I can take care of that. Take some aspirin and keep that hand iced."

"Thanks, Mr. P.," Christopher said gratefully. "I'm sure I'll be able to work tonight."

"We'll deal with that when the time comes," Mr. Passmore said.

Aisha helped him untie his apron and pack his hand in a plastic bag full of ice. She taped the end of the bag around his wrist. It felt like wearing an extremely cold baseball mitt.

They walked outside.

"Christopher," Aisha said slowly. "I've always liked to watch you work because you do it so gracefully. Because you make it seem like—like an art instead of just a job. And you always have everything perfectly under control. I've never seen you even come close to having an accident." She paused and looked up at him. "Do you want to tell me what's wrong?"

"Nothing's wrong. I just—"

"Is it Kendra?"

He sighed. "I just want her to leave," he said. This was a giant understatement. There was not a plane or bus or car or train that Christopher saw that he didn't picture Kendra on and himself waving good-bye.

Aisha shook her head slightly. "But why? She's your sister."

"I can't explain it," Christopher said.

Aisha stepped closer to him and slipped her arms around his waist. "Christopher, can't you be more generous?" She kissed his chest. "We're so lucky. We have *everything*."

Christopher kissed the top of her head. "Yes, we do," he agreed softly. *And I just want to make sure we keep it,* he thought.

Nina woke up from a dream in which she was sitting in a rocking chair and realized that she was still curled up on the bench in the boat's cabin. She checked her watch: past noon. She got up and went onto the deck.

Lucas was sitting on a small wooden chair, baiting the lobster pots. He was wearing a pair of old stained khakis and no shirt. He looked up and smiled at her. "I was just about to wake you," he said. "The sun is perfect, and I don't have anything to do but finish this and check the lines. Did you bring a swimsuit?" He gestured to a chaise-type lawn chair.

"I'm wearing my suit under my clothes," Nina said. She was suddenly embarrassed. Why hadn't she taken off her shirt and jeans in the cabin? She knew he'd only invited her because Zoey had badgered him into it. She didn't want to repay him now with the World's Least Erotic Striptease.

She began unbuttoning her shirt and was relieved when he went back to dropping bait into the traps. Still, she dreaded having him look up and see her. She was wearing her old black bikini, and normally she felt comfortable enough in it. But that was in her own backyard. What would Lucas think? She didn't have Claire's curves or Zoey's small perfection. *Oh, for heaven's sake,* Nina thought. *It's not a date. Just take off your jeans.*

She slid off her jeans and sat down on the lawn chair. Lucas looked up, and even though his glance was quick, she could tell he took in every detail of her body in the bikini. But his gaze seemed appreciative.

Nina began rubbing suntan lotion onto her shoulders. "So, who taught you how to fish?" she said.

"My dad, a long time ago," Lucas said. He smiled tightly. "Back when he still liked me. There's a bunch of guys at the marina who look out for me." He smiled again, this time a real one. "Listen, you'll like this: These four fishermen took me out for a drink yesterday, and when we were sitting around the table, I realized that I was the only one not missing a hand or an eye."

"Lucas! How terrible! Is that going to happen to you, too?"

He shook his head. "They're the kind of fishermen who deal more with hooks," he said. "I'll be fine."

Nina was lotioning her arms now. "And how's the plague of locusts?"

"The plague of whats?"

"Relatives."

"Oh. Okay, I guess. To celebrate my first day of fishing, my uncle Manny shook my hand and congratulated me on becoming a man."

Nina laughed. "Like when I first got my period and Janelle baked me a cake?"

She was so horrified that she nearly clapped her hand over her mouth. What was she thinking? This was Lucas she was talking to, not some girl. Here he was, being a good boyfriend and entertaining Zoey's friend, and here *she* was, grossing him out.

But Lucas only threw back his head and laughed. "What kind of cake?" he asked.

"It was a layer cake," Nina said shyly. "She wrote, *Good Going, Nina!* across the top in frosting."

They laughed together this time, and Nina noticed how Lucas's eyes were getting tiny laugh lines around them. Or maybe that was from squinting in the sun all day. His blond hair was bleached almost platinum.

"So, have you heard from Zoey?" he asked.

"Just a quick letter," she said. "What about you?"

"A quick letter also," he said briefly. He looked displeased, and Nina wondered why. Zoey was a wonderful writer; everyone knew that. Getting a letter from her was usually the highlight of your day.

"Hey," Lucas said, closing the last lobster pot. "I have three lobsters for you to take home. I figured you could sell them to your dad and that would help dig you out of debt a little."

"Oh, thank you!" Nina said. "Gosh, I should come with you every day. My dad might actually think I was gainfully employed."

Lucas didn't laugh, and she was mortified again. Hadn't she just reminded herself that Lucas was taking her out as a favor to Zoey a minute ago? And now she was inviting herself along again. Well, she would just have to gloss over it as best she could.

But when she looked up, Lucas was looking right at her. "Anytime you want to come on the boat with me would be wonderful, Nina," he said.

Nina couldn't say anything. She ducked her head and busied herself picking toenail polish off her big toe. She had no doubt that Lucas meant it. He didn't say things he didn't mean. *That's the cool thing about Lucas,* she thought. *You always know exactly where you stand.*

When I was blind, I always com-
plained that people treated me like an
idiot, but I've noticed that a fair
amount of them do the same thing
even now, so maybe it's just me.

Nina, for instance, thinks I don't
know how she feels. She thinks that I
didn't hear it in her voice when she
called and I was making dinner. She
wanted me to invite her. But that
wasn't all she wanted. She wanted me
to invite her, and only her, and have
some candlelight dinner and talk about
the past. She wanted to be alone with
me, watching me with her funny gray
eyes and wearing something completely inappropriate but really sexy,
like that satin slip she bought at a
thrift store and wears over her bikini
sometimes—

Oh, God. Everyone's right. I am an
idiot.

# Twelve

Jake was nervous as he rang the Cabrals' doorbell. Kate had refused to tell him any more about her strange behavior on the day he followed her. She had only cried and said that she was having a bad day. *A million bad days in a row?* Jake had wanted to ask. But Kate had said that she'd be better after a good night's sleep, and she'd agreed to go out to dinner with him tonight, so maybe everything would be okay.

He rang the doorbell again, and Kate herself answered. Her lovely red hair fell past her shoulders in thick rich waves. She wore a clingy black dress with spaghetti straps and long sparkly earrings.

Jake whistled, and Kate laughed. Maybe things would be okay after all. They hurried down the street toward the ferry.

"Where are we going?" Kate asked.

"It's a surprise," Jake said.

She smiled, but the smile didn't reach her eyes. Jake studied her eyes for a moment. Something was different about them, but he couldn't put his finger on what.

On the ferry she grew quiet, staring out at the early evening sun and water traffic as though she had never seen it before. Jake examined her profile. Her eyes did look strange. They reminded him of something, but what?

He put his face close to her ear. "What are you thinking about?"

She smiled vaguely. "Oh, just . . . the water looks so pretty."

Jake had chosen a restaurant within walking distance of the ferry landing, and when Kate saw where they were headed, she roused herself and laughed a little. "Oh, Jake, I've always wanted to eat at the Sweet Water Inn," she said.

"Now's your chance," he said, smiling, too. He would do anything to make her happy.

The hostess led them to a table with a beautiful view, and for a few moments Kate was animated, talking about the colors of the sunset and the tourists.

The waiter came to take their drink orders.

"Club soda," Jake said.

"Oh—same," Kate said.

Jake thought he saw a shadow cross her face, but he wasn't sure. The waiter handed them the menus, and Jake thought Kate looked distinctly troubled. She scanned it quickly and then closed the heavy red-and-gold book.

He tried to smile reassuringly. "Decided already?"

"Yes, I'd like the lobster bisque," she said.

Jake was puzzled. Why would someone who lived in a lobster fisherman's house want to order lobster at a restaurant? He glanced at his own menu. Lobster bisque was the first item listed under appetizers. Well, fine, he wasn't going to start cross-examining her.

"Anything else?" he said. "Want to split a main course with me?"

"No, I'm fine." She was staring out the window

again, and her blue eyes were shadowed. What was it her expression reminded him of?

The waiter came back with their drinks.

"I'll have the lobster bisque," Kate said.

"I'm sorry, miss, we are out of the lobster bisque."

Kate looked stricken.

"Perhaps I could suggest something else?" the waiter said.

Kate's mouth took on a stubborn, rebellious set. "No, forget it," she said. "I'll just have club soda."

"Not even a green salad—"

"I said forget it," Kate snapped.

Jake was shocked. He had never seen Kate be rude to anyone before, much less a waiter for something that wasn't even his fault.

"Hey," he said softly, leaning across the table to take her hand. "No need to—"

He stopped. Kate's eyes were filling with tears, and her chin was trembling.

"I'm sorry," she whispered. "Both of you—forgive me—" She stood up and ran out of the restaurant, banging her hip on a neighboring table.

Jake sat back in his chair, stunned. The waiter said something, but Jake didn't hear it. He had finally recognized the look in Kate's eyes. When he was very small, Jake's brother, Wade, was supposed to be baby-sitting and had let Jake watch a very scary movie about space aliens who took over humans' bodies. Jake remembered that movie very well because it had scared the hell out of him. But right now he was thinking about a look the aliens-in-human-disguise had had whenever they were called on to do some normal, everyday action. Their eyes had gotten a shadowed, haunted look while they tried to think of the correct behavior. Kate's eyes had the same panicked look.

After a lot of thinking, Lara decided to take flowers as a hostess gift when she went to the Passmores' for dinner. It seemed like the kind of mealymouthed present Zoey would take. She also had an envelope in her pocket with thirty dollars in it. The thirty dollars was a gamble. She couldn't afford to give it to Mr. Passmore, but she was fairly certain he'd insist she take it back.

She rang the doorbell, and Benjamin answered. He grinned his sardonic grin, and she had to smile back. She liked Benjamin.

"Enter at your own risk," he said, standing aside. "I am the primary chef tonight, so if you want to quick remember an appointment on the mainland, this would be a good time."

Lara shook her head. "I'll chance it," she said.

"Well, some people like to live dangerously, I guess," he said. He led the way into the kitchen.

Mrs. Passmore was sitting at the kitchen table, looking over some books from the restaurant. Her gaze flickered over Lara, taking in the short black skirt and white blouse. Lara didn't flinch. She'd chosen the outfit carefully. The skirt was short but not too short, and the blouse was almost schoolteacherish.

She held out the flowers to Mrs. Passmore. "These are for you," she said awkwardly.

The hard blue look that was almost always in Mrs. Passmore's eyes when she looked at Lara softened a little. "Thank you, Lara," she said. "That was very thoughtful."

Mr. Passmore walked into the kitchen, whistling. "Hello, Lara," he said pleasantly. "Just in time to help me set the table."

"Well, first I wanted to give you this," Lara said, holding out the envelope.

Mr. Passmore frowned. "What?"

*He probably thinks it's a bill from rehab,* Lara thought sourly. "It's more of the money I owe you," she said, blushing.

Mr. Passmore looked uncomfortable. "Lara, you don't need to give me money every time you see me."

Her arm was growing tired from holding out the envelope. "But I owe it to you," she said.

Mr. Passmore picked up a handful of silverware. "So you'll give me some every other time you see me," he said. "Children are allowed to pay their parents back slowly. Take Benjamin's girlfriend. How much does she owe her father?"

"Well, twenty dollars more than she did yesterday," Benjamin said in his usual sardonic tone. "The phone bill came."

"See?" Mr. Passmore gestured with the silverware. "And how fast is she paying him back?"

"I think she's averaging about a dollar a day," Benjamin said.

"There you go," Mr. Passmore said, as though this settled everything.

"Is your girlfriend coming to dinner, too?" Lara asked.

"No, not tonight," Benjamin said.

"That's too bad. I would have enjoyed seeing her," she said. That was too sweet, she thought afterward. She was sure that Benjamin, at least, would look at her sideways, but they all seemed to accept it. She supposed they were used to cloying, insincere talk from having lived with Zoey all these years. She knew she should ask about Zoey, but she couldn't bring herself to.

Instead she went to help Mr. Passmore set the table. "We're having fondue," he said.

"I've never had that," Lara said.

She was sure he would say something condescending, like, *Well, then, you're in for a treat.* But he only said, "I hope you like it. Benjamin wanted to make it."

Lara had not only never had fondue before, she wasn't entirely sure what it *was.* But it turned out to be just a big pot of boiling oil and some raw cubed meat. You speared the meat on the end of your fork and held it in the oil until it was cooked. Then there were lots of different sauces to dip the meat in.

"This was my favorite meal when I was blind," Benjamin told her as they sat down. "Because the sauces make each bite different."

Lara tasted the meat and was surprised to find that she liked it. It had seemed like a horrible dinner to her at first, like a bunch of cavemen around a fire or something. Although of course they had bread and salad, too. "So what was the worst part of being blind?" she asked Benjamin. She suspected that the question wasn't one hundred percent polite, but she wanted to know.

Benjamin looked thoughtful. "I think it was the— the insecurity," he said at last. "You know, what if I'd forgotten where the steps were? Or how many of them there were?"

"Like if you'd been daydreaming?" Lara said.

"Exactly." He smiled at her. Lara thought, *I'm having a conversation with my brother.* The thought was only slightly less amazing than if she'd suddenly found herself floating through the clouds and thought, *I'm flying.*

"Oh, no!" Mrs. Passmore cried. "Benjamin, you just pushed the meat off my fork."

"I didn't," Benjamin protested. "I was innocently minding my own business."

"Well, there it is on the bottom of the pan," Ms. Passmore said.

Lara couldn't figure out why they were making such a big deal. Why didn't Mrs. Passmore just reach down and spear it with her fork?

But Mr. Passmore was smiling. "Uh-oh. You know what that means."

"No," Lara said. "What does it mean?"

"She has to kiss all the boys."

"Why?"

"It's just a tradition that goes with fondue," Mrs. Passmore explained, putting aside her napkin. "Don't you feel sorry for me?"

But Lara could see that Mrs. Passmore was happy as she stood up and first kissed Benjamin's squirming-away face and then Mr. Passmore, who pulled her into his lap and kissed her passionately.

"Jeez," Mrs. Passmore said, patting her flushed cheeks. "I only dropped one piece."

Next it was Mr. Passmore who had the empty fork, and he kissed Mrs. Passmore more sedately this time. Lara was tense. She had never kissed her father before. But he must've sensed it because all he said was, "And an Eskimo kiss for Lara," and rubbed his nose quickly against hers.

After that they spent more time trying to push the meat off each other's forks than they did eating. Benjamin kissed his mother and Lara. Then Mr. Passmore again, and this time he kissed Lara on the cheek. She didn't mind. They were all laughing.

Lara wondered if this was what life at the Passmores' was like all the time. Was this how Benjamin and Zoey had grown up, surrounded by laughter, while she, Lara, remained a horrible little secret? The old resentments threatened to bubble up in her, but Lara wavered. She was here now, wasn't she? She was practically one of the fam—

The phone rang. Mr. Passmore leaned his chair back so far Lara thought the legs would break off and scooped up the receiver.

"Yeeeeelo," he sang into it. "Zoey! How are you, sweetheart?"

Lara was chewing on a piece of meat, and it suddenly turned to cardboard on her tongue.

"Oh, I want to speak to her, too," Mrs. Passmore said.

"Well, I've got her first," Mr. Passmore said, smiling. "You guys will just have to wait."

Lara spit the piece of meat discreetly into her napkin. She should have known that she was only having a good time because Zoey was out of town.

Mr. Passmore let out a gasp of excitement. "Way to go!" he shouted into the phone. "That's great, Zoey. Of course you should stay the extra five days." He turned to his wife and mouthed, *Zoey got the internship!*

Lara felt her stomach tighten into a hard knot. Of course perfect Zoey won the internship, or whatever it was. Sure, she'd be gone for one more week. But Zoey wouldn't stay away forever. She couldn't even let Lara have a whole evening without butting in long-distance to ruin it.

# LUCAS

I've been trying to decide which one of my relatives I'd least like to spend ten years on a desert island with. It's not an easy choice, by any means. First there's my Aunt Ginger, but she gets on my nerves so much that I'd probably pick up a club and force her into the water after a week or so.

My Aunt Luella? She'd probably talk the whole decade without stopping. Probably the rescue ship would finally heave into view and Aunt Lu would be saying, "Well, of course Manny never listens to me. I told him not to invest—oh, shoot, is the rescue ship here already?"

Uncle Manny doesn't talk, so it'd basically be like being stranded alone. I think I'd pick my uncle Joe.

Maybe he'd finally tell me what's going on. I think he'd like to.

Last night at dinner, for example. Aunt Ginger was giving my mother all these cost-cutting tips, like where to shop and stuff, and my mother said, "Clipping coupons isn't going to be enough," and A.G. said, "It'll help, and what with Lucas—" And then she broke off, and everyone else looked at their plates. Except for Uncle Joe, who looked at me with a very sad expression. What does he know? What does he know?

# Thirteen

Kate ran blindly from the restaurant. It felt as though her insides were crumbling. She could picture her heart and lungs, her ribs and spine, everything, all turning to dust and sliding down into her legs, leaving her hollow.

She ran until she reached the beach and then dropped onto the sand and curled into a ball. Tonight had taken so much out of her. It was such a Herculean effort to get dressed up and come out. So hard to concentrate on what Jake was saying.

She had held it together for as long as she could, even though she felt her control slipping. And now Jake was probably mad at her.

She curled up tighter on the damp sand and tried to think if anything in the world would make her happy right now. This was a game she played sometimes when she felt especially bad.

Let's see. . . . Would she be happy if she won the lottery? No. Who cared about money when you felt like killing yourself? Would she be happy if some fairy godmother showed up and said, You will take the best photograph of your life tomorrow? Kate wrinkled her nose. No. Would she be happy if her mother showed up and said Kate had proved she could make it on her own? No. Would she be happy if Jake proposed to her? No.

Jake's shoes appeared in her line of vision, which was about two inches off the ground. She knew they were his shoes because she could hear the sound of his breathing above her, and then the sound of him sighing. He sat down next to her in the sand.

*He's going to find out,* Kate thought. *He's going to know everything.* But she was too numb to care.

"So," Jake said, and his voice wasn't angry, just tired. "You ready to tell me what that was all about?"

Two tears squeezed out of Kate's eyes and dribbled down her cheeks into her ears. She didn't move to wipe them off. Something soft brushed her cheek. It was Jake, brushing the tears away for her with a Kleenex.

She sniffled and sat up.

"I'm depressed," she said. As soon as she said it she felt the tiniest bit less hollow. It was like a miniature puzzle piece had been fitted in somewhere in her abdomen.

"Yeah, well, I may be slow," Jake said. "But even I managed to get that much."

"I mean, I'm—I'm clinically depressed," Kate said. She looked at Jake.

He looked confused. "What does that mean?"

Kate faltered. She had never had to explain it before. "Well, it means that I'm depressed all the time, but that I can't snap out of it like normal people," she said. "It's a chemical imbalance or something. It's—it's not a matter of cheering up or whatever."

Jake cleared his throat. "It sounds like you know a lot about it," he said. There was a faint accusatory note in his voice. "You must've seen a doctor about it."

Kate was grateful that he said *doctor* and not *shrink.* "Yes, I have," she said.

"Well, is there—medicine you can take or anything?"

"Yes, sometimes I take medicine," she said quietly. "But I haven't for a long time."

Jake shifted on the sand. "And the scene at the mailbox yesterday?"

Kate studied the ground miserably. "Being clinically depressed makes it very hard to make decisions," she said.

"Like getting up in the morning?" Jake asked, but his voice wasn't sarcastic, it was interested. Kate blinked at him with her large, watery eyes.

"Yes," she said simply.

"So that explains it," he said softly, running a hand through his hair.

Kate didn't ask him what it explained. All she thought was, *He knows more than I imagined.*

"So why didn't you tell me?" Jake said. "I could have helped you."

Kate closed her eyes. *I don't deserve you,* she thought.

"I was afraid," she said.

"Afraid of what?"

Kate wanted to hug him. Here she'd been worrying that he'd never want to see her again, that he wouldn't love her if she wasn't perfect, that he wouldn't want a girlfriend with mental problems, and all he could say was, *Afraid of what?* with such genuine bewilderment in his voice.

She sighed and drew a small circle in the sand with her finger. "I haven't even told you the worst part," she said. How much stronger her voice sounded. Why hadn't she told him this before? "My mother says— well, she's very worried about me, and she says that if I can't prove I can make it on my own here that I have to move to back to New York where she can take care of me."

Jake frowned. "But she doesn't want you to drop out of school, does she?"

Kate had forgotten that Jake didn't know about the whole school fiasco. "I already dropped out of school," she said. "It just got to be—too much."

Jake nodded. He was thinking, she could see. "Well, *I* don't want you to move," he said. He put his arm around her. Kate rested her head against his shoulder. It was wonderful to have someone want her for his own selfish reasons.

Jake was still preoccupied. "Okay, well . . . first we'll have to get you back on medication. And then we'll take care of other stuff as it happens."

He turned suddenly and looked at her, a long searching look. *Here it comes,* Kate thought. *He's finally figured out that I'm mental.*

But Jake seemed satisfied with whatever he saw in her eyes. He tightened his arm around her. "Hey," he said. "I don't suppose you ever saw a movie called *Alien Invasion*?"

# Zoey

Well, I'm keeping a journal again. I'm too unhappy not to, which dovetails beautifully with my theory that unhappy people always keep diaries. Happy people are sometimes too busy running around being happy. Anne Frank is a perfect example of this. That sounds flip, and I didn't mean it to. And actually I've always kept a journal, even when Lucas used to come over every single night and I was the very happiest I ever have been.

Anyway, I just called Lucas. Here's the conversation:

Z: Hi, it's me.

L: Mmmmphump.

Z: Were you asleep?

L: Mmmmn.

Z: I just called to say I love you. I miss you. I think you're great.

L: Can you call tomorrow?

Z: You are the most incredible guy who ever lived.

L: What do the words, "I have to get up at four in the morning," mean to you?

Okay, so maybe that wasn't it exactly. But it was close enough, and you get my point. You can't love someone when you're not there. All my instincts are screaming at me to

blow off this internship
thing and to go home.
Right away. So why am I
ignoring them?

# Fourteen

Aisha pushed the heavily laden grocery cart up the aisle. Christopher was right behind her with his own similarly loaded cart, and Kendra trailed them both, checking things off the lists.

"Applesauce?" Kendra read. It was so early that they were the only people in the store, and her voice sounded unnaturally loud.

*Applesauce,* Aisha thought. *It sounds like we're in kindergarten. First applesauce, then everyone lie down on your rugs for a nap.*

She pushed the hair off her forehead. "That must be you," she said, trying to smile at Christopher.

It had been Aisha's idea to combine their grocery shopping. She and Kendra would shop for the B&B while Christopher picked up some things for Pass-mores'. Aisha had thought it would give them more time together and make the shopping go faster, too, if they were all laughing and talking. But it wasn't working out that way.

"Applesauce was back in the first aisle," Christopher said. "Why didn't you say something then?"

"Because there are about five thousand things on this list!" Kendra snapped. "What's the big deal? We'll go back and get it."

"No, *you'll* go back and get it," Christopher corrected. "Aisha and I are pushing these carts, and we're not going to go backtracking all over the place just because you were daydreaming."

Aisha saw Kendra's lips tighten, and she cringed, waiting for more harsh words. But Kendra spun on her heel and marched up the aisle, the hem of her short summer skirt swaying angrily.

"Once I dropped a jar of spaghetti sauce in the supermarket," Aisha said softly. "And I was trying to sort of move away casually when all of a sudden this voice came over the loudspeaker: *Cleanup in aisle ten!* It was horrible."

Christopher wasn't listening. He was still fuming and looking crossly in the direction Kendra had gone.

Aisha kept her voice light. "And I knew this guy once who worked in supermarket surveillance, and he used to watch people dump sand out of the seats of their swimsuits when they thought they were all alone."

He still wasn't listening to her.

"Christopher," Aisha said. "This is a trip to the supermarket, okay? It's not the military, we're not invading Kuwait, all right? If Kendra doesn't read every item on the list in precise order, nothing horrible is going to happen."

"I just don't want to be here all day," Christopher said. "She's so disorganized."

Aisha rolled her eyes. "So she's disorganized! She's sixteen years old! Can't you cut her some slack?"

"I do—"

"You don't!" Aisha interrupted. "You are on her about every little thing, every minute of the day, and I don't understand it. I work with her all day long, and I'm never even tempted to yell at her. She gets to work more or less on time, she's a quick study, she keeps me company, she makes me laugh. She's great, Christopher, that's what she is, and you treat her like—like—" She paused. "Aren't you going to say anything?"

"I'm waiting for you to finish."

She sighed. "I guess I'm pretty much done."

"Aren't you going to say what it is I treat Kendra like?"

"No, because I can't think of the right word," Aisha said absently. Her anger was vanishing. "Can't you just be *nice* to her?"

Christopher looked uncomfortable. "She gets on my nerves," he said. "It's like trying to explain why you don't like broccoli."

"But she's not a vegetable. She's your sister," Aisha insisted.

Christopher smiled wryly. "Okay, I get your point. I'll be nicer."

"But that's *not* my point," Aisha said. "I think if you just made the effort, you might actually like her."

Christopher raised an eyebrow. "Don't count on it."

"But what's not to like?" Aisha shook her head. "She thinks the world of you. She was telling me yesterday about the Halloween when your mother couldn't afford any costumes and you made her a princess crown—"

"What else has she told you?" Christopher barked. His face was thunderous.

Aisha was startled. "Nothing in particular. What's wrong with that? I *loved* that story, Christopher." She put her hand on his arm. "It made me love you even more. Can't you see that only good things can come from everyone getting along?"

He didn't answer, still looking angry and preoccupied. Then his expression cleared a little, and he looked down at her. He put his large hand over hers. "The last thing I want to do is fight with you about Kendra," he said. "If you want me to be nicer to her, I'll try."

Aisha smiled at him.

"Where do you think she is, anyway?" Christopher asked.

Aisha had practically forgotten that Kendra was even in the store with them. "Gosh, I don't know," she said, glancing around. "Maybe she went out to sulk in the car."

"Well, I'll go apologize to her," Christopher said, "but first I want to kiss you."

"Kiss me?" Aisha said. Her voice squeaked.

"Yes, kiss you," Christopher said, putting his arms around her.

"Right here in frozen foods?"

"Right here in frozen foods."

Aisha giggled and put her arms around his neck. They kissed in the showy, passionate way of movie stars, Christopher bending her back over the freezer until the ends of her hair brushed the TV dinners.

The Passmores' house was almost completely silent in the midmorning lull, with Mr. and Mrs. Passmore at the restaurant already and Benjamin not out of bed yet. In fact, it would have been *completely* silent except that Nina was also in the bed that Benjamin had not gotten out of, and they were a happy tangle of arms and legs.

Part of Nina felt like singing every time Benjamin touched her. He kissed her collarbone, drawing an involuntary moan from her, and she thought, *He loves me! He wants me!* But part of her, an always cynical part, thought, *I wish we were talking instead of making out.*

Benjamin pulled her on top of him, running his hands down her back. Nina told the cynical part of her to shut up. She concentrated on kissing Benjamin. But he must've sensed something because he pulled away and studied her face.

"Is something wrong?"

She hesitated. If she said, *I'd like more talking and less making out,* she would sound like a prude. She would sound as though she didn't like making out, as though she only did it as some sort of—of reward for Benjamin after he'd talked to her enough. And that wasn't it at all. Nina loved making out with Benjamin. It was only that she hadn't seen him all week and now that she was finally with him, she wanted *more* than just making out.

"I've—I've missed you," she said finally.

"I've missed you, too," Benjamin said, pulling her back down. But Nina could tell from the urgent way his lips sought hers that he didn't miss her in quite the same way.

"Benjamin," she said abruptly, breaking the kiss. He was busy unbuttoning her shirt. She rebuttoned the shirt just as quickly, which made them both laugh.

"Okay, Nina," Benjamin said. "Here." He slid her off him and settled her in the crook of his arm. "Now, let's talk."

She laughed. "How did you know that's what I was thinking?"

"Because I'm not a complete toad, as I believe you once said." He ran his hand along her body, and his voice got huskier. "What shall we talk about?"

Nina laughed. "Stop being impossible."

"I'm not being impossible," Benjamin said, starting to kiss her again. "I'm being interested, I'm being

104

attentive." He looked at Nina's wide gray eyes and turned serious again. "What is it?"

She shifted uncomfortably. "Well, just what we were saying before? About missing each other?"

"Uh-huh."

"Well . . . why should we miss each other, Benjamin?" She sat up, straightening her blouse. "I mean, we live two blocks from each other! It's summer; we have lots of time."

Benjamin rolled onto his back and groaned. "Nina, I called and asked you to come over because I wanted to be with you," he said. "Not because I wanted to have some boring relationship-type fight about how we don't see each other enough."

Nina's temper flared. "You didn't ask me over because you wanted to be with me! You wanted to fool around with me!"

Benjamin remained maddeningly calm. "What's wrong with that? You're my girlfriend, aren't you?"

"Am I?" Nina shot back. *Oh, God,* she thought. *Why did I say that? What if he says no?*

But he didn't say no. He said, "Yes, of course, you're my girlfriend," and gathered her into his arms again. "Nina, let's not fight."

"Okay," she said moodily against his chest. She felt like fighting. She felt like having a big, rip-roaring shouting match.

But she said nothing and let Benjamin begin kissing her again.

*He's impatient,* she thought. *He's always so impatient now. He was never like this before.*

But soon Benjamin's hands and lips had made Nina impatient, too, and she felt almost happy. She loved Benjamin, and she'd rather be with him—on any terms—than not at all.

# Claire

I miss Aaron. I wish he didn't sleep at his friends' houses all the time. I wish he could tell how much I need him to be here now. How could I feel scared if Aaron were right down the hall—or right in my room? If Aaron were here, would I have done something so totally dumb and childish as cutting that photograph right out of Nina's true-crime book? Well, it doesn't matter. He's not here. And he's not going to be here. Not until whatever he finds so interesting on the mainland stops being so interesting.

Oh, I forgot the weather. High-pressure system holding. Cold front coming from east is blocked by high-pressure ridge

106

and is producing some fog well to the south. Here it's clear, though. You could see for miles. If you were spying on someone, you could see them perfectly.

# Fifteen

Jake went with Kate to the pharmacy, and she was grateful. Even though this errand was the only thing she would do all day, she knew she would spend the rest of the day in bed. It wasn't because she was sleepy; it was because the trip mentally exhausted her. And so she was grateful for Jake—his presence guaranteed that she would actually stay and pick up her medication.

They walked up to the counter. "Um, a Dr. Ramsey . . . from New York was supposed to . . . call in a prescription for me," Kate said falteringly. Jake squeezed her hand.

"Last name, please?"

"Oh—Levin," Kate answered, feeling foolish.

The pharmacist flipped through a file box. "Here we are," he said. "It'll be at least forty-five minutes. We're busy today."

She went and sat down next to Jake in the minuscule waiting area.

At first Jake tried to entertain her. "Let's make up the life story of these other people," he whispered. "What do you think that old lady does?"

Kate looked, but all she could see was a nondescript elderly woman in a blue Windbreaker. She would leave imagination to other people. Just basic, ordinary, mundane thinking was all Kate could handle. "I don't know," she said listlessly.

"Come on," Jake coaxed. "I bet she's a drug fiend and she stole her doctor's prescription pad and every day she has to go to a different pharmacy so they won't recognize her."

Kate tried to rouse herself and smile faintly. She looked at Jake and felt a wave of gratitude. How much fun could this be for him? *What did you do today? . . . Oh, I went to the pharmacy with my depressed girlfriend. It was a blast.*

Jake seemed to sense that she wasn't up to talking, and he simply curled up contentedly in the chair next to her, somehow managing to exude the appearance that this was a normal morning for him, that there weren't a thousand other things he'd rather be doing.

Kate, meanwhile, felt like a bundle of knots. She'd been on antidepressants before. She knew the side effects: weight gain, acne, irritability. True, she didn't always have the side effects, but still, why did she even have to take antidepressants? Other people didn't. Other people just got up in the morning and went about their normal business.

Jake didn't understand. "Diabetics have to take insulin," he'd said last night. "You have to take antidepressants. What's the difference?" Kate thought there was a huge difference, but somehow she couldn't put it into words.

Kate sighed. She looked down and began picking at each of her cuticles, not stopping until there was a raw, bloody crescent around each fingernail. If Jake noticed, he didn't stop her. She was on the sixth finger when he touched her arm gently and said, "It's been an hour."

Kate was startled. An hour? In a way it seemed much shorter. In a way much longer. She went back to the pharmacy counter, and the pharmacist told her that it would be at least another forty-five minutes.

Kate went back to Jake. "It's going to take another hour, I guess," she said.

He looked uncomfortable. "The thing is," he said apologetically, "I sort of planned on going to an A.A. meeting. Will you be okay?"

Before she could stop herself, it flashed across Kate's mind that he was lying. *He doesn't have to go to a meeting,* she thought crankily. *He's just tired of hanging out in the pharmacy with a nutcase.*

Immediately she tried to smooth the thoughts down. She knew that paranoia was a symptom of depression. "Sure, I'll be fine," she said, trying to muster a smile.

*What a pair we are,* she thought. *Sure, honey, you run along to your A.A. meeting, and I'll stay here for my mood-altering drugs.*

Jake gave her his old flippant grin. "Don't talk to any strange men."

"You're the only man I want to talk to," Kate responded automatically, but it didn't sound playful and reassuring. It sounded, she thought, needy and clingy. *You're the only man I want. I need you. Don't leave me. I'll crack up if you do.*

But Jake's smile didn't waver. He kissed her, whispered, "I love you," in her ear, and left.

Fifteen minutes later a girl at the pharmacy counter called Kate's name.

"Now, have you taken antidepressants before?" she asked loudly.

Kate cringed, nodding. Did this girl have to tell the whole store?

"Remember it's important to take it every five hours

with food," the girl was saying. "That may mean you have to change your meal schedule."

Kate was still nodding numbly. Hadn't she just told this girl she'd taken them before? She took the familiar brown bottle with its green cap and white label. She slipped it into her pocket, wondering if she would ever take a single pill.

She had turned to go when the girl said, "Hey, can I ask you something?" *Here we go,* Kate thought. *She's going to tell me all about her mother or sister or friend who's been depressed.*

She looked at the girl. She hadn't been on duty when Kate and Jake first got there. "What?" she said indifferently.

The girl leaned her elbows on the counter. "Didn't you used to go out with Jake McRoyan?" she asked.

"I still do," Kate said, wondering how much longer this would be true.


"I don't understand why I have to run these stupid errands just because you're in debt up to your eyeballs," Claire said to Nina as they walked down the street.

Nina was reading her list. "Um—because you're my sister and you love me? Oh, wait, that doesn't really apply, does it? Actually the real reason is because I'll need help carrying stuff from the grocery store."

Claire gave her a scornful look. "How much is Janelle paying you, anyway?"

"Fifty cents per stop," Nina said, "and don't try laying some sob story on me about how you want your fair share."

"It is way beneath my dignity to beg and plead for my fair share of fifty cents," Claire said. "Although I do think I'm going above and beyond the call of duty.

You know perfectly well you could have had the grocery store deliver if you'd called them earlier instead of scampering off to have some good-morning grope with Benjamin."

"It wasn't a good-morning grope!" Nina said hotly.

Claire smiled faintly. "What was it, then?"

"None of your business," Nina said. "Look, we've walked right past the cleaner's."

"Don't change the subject," Claire said, but Nina had already turned around to retrace their steps. She darted into the dry cleaner, and by the time Claire entered the shop, she was at the counter giving her ticket to the assistant.

"Nina—" Claire said, and then stopped as the bell above the door jangled. Mrs. Cabral entered.

There was a beat of silence, and then Claire said, "Hello, Mrs. Cabral."

Mrs. Cabral grunted.

"Hi," Nina said. "I'm awfully sorry to hear about your husband."

*Now why didn't I say that?* Claire wondered.

"Thank you," Mrs. Cabral said stiffly. She drummed her fingers on the counter for the attendant. Claire and Nina left awkwardly.

"She hates me," Claire said once they were out on the street.

"Well, she didn't exactly fall all over me, either," Nina said.

But Claire didn't answer. She was wondering if Mrs. Cabral hated her enough to send her anonymous photographs. Maybe. Maybe the death of her husband had pushed her into action.

She followed Nina into the hardware store, where Nina entered into some astonishingly boring conversation about nails with Mr. Benson. *What about Lucas?*

Claire thought. *He must hate me. He'd be an idiot not to, after all he's been through. And now he's spending all that time on the fishing boat, with nothing to do but plot revenge. . . .*

Nina bought the nails, and they walked back onto the street. Sarah Mendel whipped by in her island car and honked. "Hello, girls!" she called out the window.

Both Claire and Nina waved. But Claire suddenly felt suspicious. Had Sarah ever *really* forgiven Claire for trying to break up her marriage numerous times? Sarah was home most days. It would be easy for her to sneak out and put an envelope in the mailbox. That would explain the lack of a postmark, too.

They walked past Passmores', and Claire turned to Nina suddenly. "Do you think Mr. and Mrs. Passmore hate me?"

Nina rolled her eyes. "Why would they?"

"Well, because I broke Benjamin's heart, and I haven't always been that nice to Zoey—"

"Now, there's an overstatement and an understatement," Nina said cheerfully. "The overstatement is that you did *not* break Benjamin's heart. He's too smart for that. The understatement is that you haven't always been 'that nice' to Zoey. But either way, why are you being so paranoid? You think every single person we meet is out to get you today."

*Well, someone* is *out to get me,* Claire thought, but she didn't say anything. Nina was probably right. She *was* paranoid, thinking all sorts of people hated her, people who probably never gave her a second thought.

She and Nina went into the bookstore. "I'll meet you by the cash register," Claire said. "I want to get a copy of *Vogue.*"

She walked to the back of the store, feeling a little better. Then she froze.

Mr. McRoyan was in the aisle, reading a copy of *Car and Driver.* Claire remembered suddenly that Wade had liked cars, too, but Jake didn't. She wondered absently why her brain had chosen to supply her with this bit of information. She felt hot. Her forehead was clammy. Mr. McRoyan looked up and saw her, but before he could say anything, Claire fled.

She ran past Nina, past the cash register, out onto the sidewalk, where she stood, shaking and badly out of breath. It wasn't that Mr. McRoyan had looked sad or angry or lonely. It was just that Claire had realized that there *were* people who hated her and probably always would.

# Aisha

My mother baked this casserole
and forced me to take it over to
Lucas's today. Actually it's a
delicious casserole, one of my
favorites, but I felt dumb, handing it to Mrs. Cabral. Here's a
casserole, I know your husband
just died and all, but maybe a little ham and pasta will do wonders
for you. (Although before I was
even out the door, I saw Lucas's
uncle eating a big spoonful)

Anyway, Mrs. Cabral said to
tell my mom thanks, and I said
I would, and then she said,
"Aren't you the one who's
engaged?" I said yes, and one of
Lucas's aunts swooped down on
me and showed me pictures of her
daughter's wedding for fifteen
minutes. (That is something I'll
never do now that I know how
boring it is) And then Lucas's

aunt asked me if my hope chest
was ready. A hope chest! Like I
need all this equipment or something. I just need to find out
what's going on. I just need
Christopher to tell me the truth.

# Sixteen

Nina was actually hoping that she wouldn't see anyone she knew on the ferry ride home from the hair salon. She was mentally devising a way to tie bricks to her bangs to make them grow faster.

Still, her spirits rose a little when Lucas spotted her and waved. Talking to him always cheered her up. *Besides,* she thought as he sat down beside her, *he might not even notice my haircut.* Benjamin certainly wouldn't.

"Hey, you got a haircut," Lucas said immediately, dashing that hope.

"I got them all cut," Nina teased, trying to change the subject.

But Lucas was studying her bangs. "It's—" He hesitated.

"*Short?*" Nina prompted. "Is that the word that springs to mind?"

"Well—yes," Lucas admitted.

Nina sighed.

"Did you ever see *An American in Paris?*" Lucas asked.

"No."

"Well, you should. Leslie Caron's bangs might make you feel better."

"Look, at this point an army recruitment poster

117

would make me feel better," Nina said. "But that's not saying much."

Lucas laughed.

"Hey, why aren't you out on the fishing boat, anyway?" Nina asked suddenly.

Lucas grimaced. "I needed an engine part from the mainland. That's another day lost."

"Well, I'm glad you're here," Nina said. "I'm going to be lonely enough next year, riding the ferry by myself every single day."

Lucas looked at her. "You're really dreading next year, aren't you?"

"Are you kidding?" Nina said. "I keep having these nightmares about spending all my time at the Weymouth bowling alley because I won't have any friends. In the spring they'll find my frozen body by the railroad tracks and all the regulars will say, 'She was just lookin' for the ladies' room.'"

Lucas looked stunned. "Jesus, Nina," he said. "Don't get so carried away. Besides, the odds are that I'll still be here with you next year."

"Oh, Lucas, no!" Nina felt so sorry for him that she momentarily forgot her own fears. "You mean you won't be able to go to college?"

He shook his head. "My mom keeps talking like I will, but I don't see how. She doesn't have a job. All we have right now is my income from the boat."

"But that's so unfair!" Nina said.

Lucas shrugged. "Maybe. But I don't have a choice."

The ferry was pulling up to the landing, and they both stood up. Nina wished she knew what to say. She didn't think it would be of enormous consolation to Lucas if she said, *Well, at least we can still hang out together.*

118

The ferry docked, and the gates clanged down. She and Lucas hurried to get off. Lucas automatically reached for Nina's hand to help her onto the dock, the same way she'd seen him do with Zoey a hundred times.

She took his hand lightly, dropping it the second she stepped onto the dock. A woman near them watched the whole encounter, smiling approvingly at Lucas.

*She thinks he's my boyfriend,* Nina realized suddenly. She looked at him out of the corner of her eye and noticed again how deeply tanned he was, how the days spent doing hard work in the sun were making him look older and more handsome. She was very flattered that someone would think he was her boyfriend.

She thought of something and laughed out loud.

"What's so funny?" Lucas asked.

"Oh, I'll tell you some other time," Nina said.

She had actually been thinking that Lucas had made her feel something that she had thought would be impossible, at least until her bangs grew out: beautiful.

Lara looked for an empty seat in the A.A. meeting. Jake saw her before she saw him, but she caught his glance in time to notice the appreciative look he gave, and she smiled in return. She knew she looked good in her blue-striped River Island shirt and short shorts. Her reduced drinking had sharpened her facial features, making her cheekbones seem more prominent and her eyes larger. Her boyishly short platinum hair contrasted with the lushness of her figure.

Yes, Lara was pleased with the picture she presented. And she was equally pleased with the favorable look from Jake. Especially considering the fact that the last time she'd spoken to him, he'd still been angry at her for running his precious Kate off the road on the way to prom.

*Part of the problem with A.A.*, Lara thought, *is that there are not enough boys.* It was even worse than high school, which was boring, but at least there was dating potential.

She sat down next to Jake. "Hi, handsome."

"Hello," Jake said neutrally.

Lara shrugged. Let him be impersonal; he would still report to Mr. Passmore that she'd been at the meeting. Or maybe he wouldn't. He was just the kind to respect the confidentiality rule.

She crossed her well-muscled, lightly tanned legs, and Jake watched. Lara smiled.

"It's good to see you here," Jake said at last, with an effort.

"It's always good to see you," Lara said.

"No, I mean, here, getting the help you need."

She shrugged. "I don't need this. Only drunks need this."

Jake smiled faintly. "Then why do you always lick your lips during the meetings?"

"I do no such thing."

"Whatever you say."

Lara stopped paying attention to Jake. The meeting was about to begin, and she liked the first part of every meeting. This actually was more interesting than school, where the teachers were always droning on about history or math or something. In an A.A. meeting there was always some poor slob who stood up and told the always fascinating story of how alcohol had ruined his or her life. Lara thought most of the speakers were fools, but she enjoyed their stories.

Tonight the speaker was a middle-aged man with a red face. He said that he was the shop teacher at a local high school. He told how he used to drink a bottle of Asti-Spumonti every morning (at this point a sort of happy, thirsty sigh went around the room). Anyway, he had the usual number of incidents: minor car accidents, missing money, drunken scenes. Lara leaned forward, waiting for the turning point. One day the shop teacher cut off his own finger with the jigsaw— "The *what?*" Lara whispered to Jake—and was so drunk that he didn't feel anything. He just watched the blood spurt from his hand and stared at the dismembered finger lying on the floor until one of his students called an ambulance. And that, said the shop teacher, was his "wake-up call," and he'd joined A.A. and hadn't had a drink in six years.

*Aha!* Lara thought. He'd cut off his finger *eight* years ago, which meant that he'd fallen off the wagon at least once.

But of course no one else noticed; they all clapped like mad. Lara noticed that the shop teacher had all his fingers, and she wanted to ask about how the severed finger had been sewn back on and—more important— how did they get it to the hospital? Did a student just put it in his backpack or what?

Instead the meeting went into its second half, where they talked about the twelve steps and taking things one day at a time and blah, blah, blah. Lara spent this part of the meeting studying the A.A. creed and seeing how many words she could make out of "Perseverance."

Before she knew it, the meeting was over.

"So what did you think?" Jake asked.

Lara did a quick tally. "Thirty-seven words," she said. "Which is three more than last week."

Jake gave her a scornful look. "Why do you come if you think it's such a crock?"

Lara stood up and stretched. "Because I want to stay out of rehab, and this was part of the deal with Zoey's father."

"Why do you call him that?"

"What else am I supposed to call him? Dad?" Lara laughed shortly.

"Well, why not? I'm sure he'd love it."

Lara's lips tightened. "No, he loves being Zoey's dad too much," she said. "And I don't think he likes being Lara's dad at all."

They walked out of the church into the bright afternoon. Lara wondered why everything always seemed bright and fresh and clean after an A.A. meeting. Was it because they always held the meetings in such dark, cigarette-smelling places?

Still, she was in a good mood. She didn't have to go to another meeting for a whole week. She tossed her head so that her lapis earrings danced.

Jake was still walking beside her.

"Hey," Lara said suddenly, "do you want to go get a drink?"

He looked at her.

She rolled her eyes. "I mean a *beverage*," she said. "Coke? Coffee? Yoo-Hoo? Chicken broth?"

Jake's gaze suddenly focused on something beyond her, and his eyes were so plaintive that Lara felt a pang. If only someone would look at her that way.

"No, thanks," Jake said brusquely. "I've got to go."

He hurried away, and Lara knew before she turned what she would see. She was right. A slight, redheaded girl, standing on the corner, staring at the ground. And Jake hurrying to put his arms around her.

# Nina

So this morning at breakfast
my dad, who can really be a dork
sometimes, starts giving Claire
this big hearty talk about how
when you're away at college, it
makes all the difference just
knowing you can come home anytime you want. All the difference in whether you're homesick
or not, is what he meant.

Then he turned to me and
said, "Nina, I know you're going
to be logging a lot of hours
crying your eyes out in your
room next year, but I think it
would make all the difference if
Benjamin knows he can see you

whenever he wants. Not that
he will, of course."

I'm kidding. He didn't say
that. But he could have. He was
thinking it, I'm sure. We all
were, even me, while a tear fell
into my oatmeal.

# Seventeen

Jake was sure to make plenty of noise as he raced up to Kate, but even so she jumped about a foot when he touched her.

"Hey, beautiful," he whispered into the back of her neck, holding her tightly, trying to calm her.

*How could she not have heard me?* he wondered. *What does she think about when she withdraws into herself like that? Where does she go?*

"Talk about perfect timing," he said, releasing her. "Or have you been waiting here a long time?"

Kate checked her watch, but Jake already knew by the blank look in her eyes that she had no idea whether she'd been waiting twenty seconds or twenty minutes.

"Not—not too long," she said at last.

Jake smiled at her. "Well," he said. "Here we are with the rest of the day before us and"—he pulled the change out of his pocket and counted it—"all of a dollar thirty-five to spend. What would you like to do?"

Kate got that panicky look again, and he remembered that she didn't like to make decisions. "Walk?" she said quickly. "Could we just walk a little?"

"Sure," Jake said, taking her hand.

"In—in silence?"

"If that's what you'd like."

She didn't say anything else, and quietly they walked up the street. Suddenly Kate said, "It's not that I don't like talking to you—"

"Hey," Jake protested, teasing. "You didn't even last ten seconds."

"I'm serious," Kate said, her voice wavering. "I love talking to you, but it—makes me tired. Everything makes me so tired."

"Will the medication help?"

"I guess so," she said wearily, and he didn't say anything more.

He noticed that they were walking directly back to the ferry. He grimaced inwardly. Kate obviously wanted to get back home where she could stare at her computer or her television or thin air and think about nothing. Well, that was okay because he wanted to go to the library this afternoon and look up some information about clinical depression. He wanted to know everything so he could help her through this. The idea of going to the library cheered him up enough that he lifted her hand and kissed it impulsively.

Kate rewarded him with a faint smile, and just at that moment Jake caught a flash of pale hair behind him.

"Excuse me," Lara said, passing them on the narrow sidewalk. Her voice was pleasant enough, but Jake saw the hard glint in her eyes as she looked at Kate. He couldn't blame Kate at all for shrinking against him.

He put an arm around her. Lara was in front of them, her tanned legs striding purposefully. A gray plastic bag dangled from her hand, and Jake heard a sound that he would have known anywhere: bottles clinking together.

He frowned. *It could be soda,* he told himself hopefully. *It could be juice. It could be—what else comes in bottles?*

He was kidding himself. He knew all too well what came in bottles, as did Lara. Beer, wine, vodka, scotch, whiskey, bourbon, gin. To name a few.

Lara tossed them one last, appraising look over her shoulder before she turned the corner and disappeared from sight.

Jake was still preoccupied by the clinking sound from Lara's bag. He glanced at Kate. She looked pale and uneasy. His concern deepened. Lara sober was bad enough for Kate, but Lara drunk was a disaster waiting to happen. Jake thought suddenly of the time Lara had run Kate off the road.

His arm tightened around the frail girl next to him. He would protect her. That was all there was to it. But a small voice in the back of his mind spoke up. *Are you sure? Can you protect her* all *the time? What happens if you can't?*

Kate was looking at him. "What are you thinking?" she said suddenly.

"Nothing important."

"No, tell me," she said.

Jake sighed. Why did Kate have to pick this particular moment to snap out of her haziness and start questioning him?

"I was just thinking that, well, I hope North Harbor *is* the right place for you," he said awkwardly. As soon as he said the words he wanted to take them back, but it was too late.

Benjamin looked at the pretty girl in the grocery store for a full thirty seconds before he realized it was Nina. She was wearing a faded black bikini he'd never seen before. It clung to her body in a way that made it difficult to remember that everyone always said Claire was the sexier Geiger sister. She was leaning against the counter, every bit as carefree as if she were in her own bedroom and chattering to Mr. Weinglass in a light, happy voice.

"Hello, Nina," Benjamin said.

She spun around. "Benjamin!" Her face lit up.

But then, oddly, neither of them seemed to know what to say. Benjamin remembered making out with her just a few hours ago and felt ashamed. It was like meeting a girl he'd had a one-night stand with. But that was crazy. This was *Nina*.

He noticed that she was staring at him with an expectant look.

"So, um, how are things going?" he said awkwardly.

She looked at him sourly. "As well as can be expected without bangs," she said.

Oh, so that was it. She had wanted him to notice her haircut. He looked closer. Now that she pointed it out, he could see that her bangs were shorter (well, almost nonexistent). He could see all of her eyebrows. But that was okay; she had nice eyebrows: thin, arched, expressive.

"You don't like them?" he said at last.

"It's hard to like something that's not there," she said. Her voice was flippant, but Benjamin felt a twisting in his stomach. Was she talking about her bangs—or him?

In the next sentence, though, she was laughing and talking about the guy who cut her hair. "I went to him because Claire and I used to go together and get our hair cut by this guy named Ramon?" She said it like a question, so Benjamin nodded, even though he didn't know who Ramon was.

"Anyway, last time Claire went first, and Ramon kept saying, *You have the loveliest hair, just the right amount of natural curl.*" Nina was doing Ramon's voice and Benjamin could hear it: overconfident, condescending, professional. "And then it was my turn

128

and he said, *Nina, I see you have some dandruff.* I kept saying, *Okay, I'll get some shampoo, don't worry about it,* but he couldn't stop talking. *Oh, it's nothing to be ashamed of, Nina.* I thought Claire would never stop laughing."

By this time Benjamin and even Mr. Weinglass behind the counter were laughing.

"So that's why I went to this other guy," Nina said, smiling a little.

There was another awkward pause, and then she turned back to Mr. Weinglass. "Let's see," she said thoughtfully. "I'd like two coffees with milk, half a pound of potato salad, and a ham sandwich. But tell me when you get to the ham sandwich because I have pretty specific instructions."

"Sure thing," Mr. Weinglass said, still grinning. He set about gathering her other items behind the counter.

"Where are you going?" Benjamin asked.

"Oh, I just ran into Lucas on the ferry and we're going out on his father's boat," she said. "I thought I'd bring lunch."

"I'm ready, Nina," Mr. Weinglass called from down by the deli case.

Nina pattered down and stood on tiptoe to talk over the glass. Her fingers drummed absently against her flat stomach.

"I want a little bit of mustard on one side of the roll and then a little bit of mayo on the other," she said. "Use Black Forest ham and cut it pretty thin. And I want lettuce and tomato, but not very much tomato."

Suddenly Benjamin felt very left out. Nina was his girlfriend; why wasn't she buying food for a picnic with *him?* That was irrational; he knew Nina would like to see him much more than she did. But he couldn't shake the feeling.

Mr. Weinglass rang up Nina's purchases, and Benjamin walked out with her.

"Didn't you get anything?" she asked.

"I lost my appetite," he said shortly.

Nina checked her watch. "Well, I'd better get going," she said. "What are you doing this afternoon? Photography class or something?"

Actually Benjamin did have photography class, but he resented Nina referring to it so casually, like, *You go on with your photography class; I have to go meet Lucas.*

"Yes," he said coolly.

Nina looked at him. "What's your problem?"

He shrugged. "You sure seem to know how Lucas likes his sandwiches," he said. Anger nudged him. "You couldn't just take him any old ham sandwich, could you? Lucas likes Black Forest ham, Lucas doesn't want too much tomato—" He broke off when he saw her face. She was pale, with two flaming spots of color on each cheek.

"For your information," she said furiously, "I have no idea how Lucas likes his sandwiches. That is how I like *my* sandwiches. I was ordering it to *my* specifications, which is something you might know about me if you had any interest in me at all. Except when you're being a pig who's just jealous because someone else is being nice to me, that is!" She was breathing heavily. "Screw you, Benjamin! Go to your stupid class! Normally I can't keep you away from it."

She turned and marched angrily down the street.

Benjamin watched her until she was out of sight, thinking that the straight, proud set of her narrow shoulders was the saddest thing he'd seen since he got his vision back.

# Eighteen

*"Hi, this is Nina, and I'm not going anywhere until my bangs grow out, but please leave a message, anyway."* Beep.

"Hi, Nina, this is Lucas, and, uh, regardless of your bang situation, I just wanted to make sure you, and, uh, Benjamin, were going to Aaron's show tomorrow at the Sand Bar. Give me a call."

*"Hello, this is the Passmores'."* Beep.

"Wow, I like the new no-frills message. This is Nina, calling for Benjamin, but I guess he's out doing more interesting things than waiting for the phone to ring. I'm just wondering if he's going to the show in Portland tomorrow, and, um, if he'd like to go with me. If he's still speaking to me. Call me."

*"Hello, this is the Passmores'."* Beep.

"Hello, this is Nina again. I just wanted to call back and clarify that Benjamin should only call me if he's still speaking to me. . . . Otherwise, it would be kind of pointless. Plus Claire would think it was the crank caller."

*"Hello, you've reached the Cabral residence. Please leave your name and a brief message."* Beep.

"Kate? Kate, it's Jake. I know you're home because I just walked by and saw your light on. . . . Well, I guess you're not going to pick up the phone. I'm calling to see if you want to go to Aaron's show. Give me a call if you feel up to it."

*"Hello, please leave a message for Christopher—[in the background] and Kendra!—for* Christopher. *Thank you very much."* Beep.

"Hello, Christopher and Kendra. This is Aisha, wondering if one or both of you want to go to Aaron's show tomorrow. Call me."

*"Hi, this is Zoey, and I'm not home. Unless you're a burglar, in which case I'm really here with a steak knife and a Doberman. Either way, leave a message."* Beep.

"Zo, it's me. Sorry I missed you. I just wanted to congratulate you again on winning the internship. And I wanted to hear the sound of your voice. Good night."

*"Hi, this is Nina and I'm not going anywhere until my bangs grow out, but please leave a message, anyway."* Beep.

"Oh, what happened to your bangs? You didn't have them cut by that new guy in Weymouth, did you? He cut my mom's hair and she *cried*, which I don't remember her ever doing before. Anyway, this is Aisha, and I'm just calling to see if you and Claire want to go to Aaron's show, which I guess you probably know about, seeing as how you live right in the same house with him and all. Give me a call."

*"Hello, this is the Gray residence. If you wish to make a reservation or speak to a guest, please press one now." Beep.*

"Eesh, this is Kendra. Christopher and I would love to go to the show tomorrow. Christopher can't tell you that right now because he's too busy being irritable with me. But I can't wait. Talk to you tomorrow."

*"Hi, this is Zoey, and I'm not home. Unless you're a burglar, in which case I'm really here with a steak knife and a Doberman. Either way, leave a message." Beep.*

"It's not a burglar; it's me, Nina! Here I am plunging myself further into debt by calling you long-distance, and you're not even home. What's going on? Is it true you're abandoning us for yet another week? I suppose you're out being all urban and cosmopolitan. Call me when you can."

*"Hi, this is Nina, and I'm not going anywhere until my bangs grow out, but please leave a message, anyway." Beep.*

"Nina, it's Dad. I just got my MasterCard bill, and I have a feeling that your bangs may be the least of your problems. Please be home when I get there."

*"Hello, you've reached the Cabral residence. Please leave your name and a brief message."* Beep.

"Hi, this is Zoey calling for Lucas. I'm sorry I missed your call. I want to hear your voice, too. I guess you're probably already asleep. I would tell you how much I miss you, but then this message wouldn't be brief, although it's probably not brief even without me saying how I miss you. I will definitely talk to you tomorrow. Love, Zoey. Oh, jeez, that was dumb! This isn't a letter; I don't have to *sign* it. But I do love you, so I'll leave that on there. Love, Zoey."

*"Hi, this is the Geiger residence, Claire speaking. If you've tried to call earlier, you may have thought you had the wrong machine, due to a certain inconsiderate individual with unfortunate bangs. However, please feel free to leave a message now."* Beep.

"Um, hi, this is a message for Aaron. Tell him that I will definitely be at his show tomorrow and that I can't wait to see him. Oh, I forgot to say my name. This is Mia."

Claire listened to the message and then rewound the tape.

# Nineteen

## 9:00 a.m.

Aisha was helping Kendra make a bed and silently vowing never to have a career in hotel management. She and Kendra pulled the bedspread taut and stood up, breathless.

Kendra checked her watch. "Forty seconds," she said. It was a new record for them.

Aisha looked at Kendra and suddenly thought, *She knows something.* It was a strange notion, and she had no idea where it came from.

## 10:00 a.m.

Nina was doing the family laundry (for fifty cents per load) and hoping that tonight she could patch things up with Benjamin.

Sarah, Nina's stepmother, standing nervously by, said, "Are you sure you know what you're doing?"

"Of course I do," Nina said cheerfully. "I'm not a complete idiot, you know."

## 11:00 a.m.

Lucas, who had been up for six hours already, was pulling wet rope aboard the boat. Salt water scoured the dozens of tiny cuts on his hands. Lucas's lips tightened. He was definitely going to the show even if it meant he'd be a zombie tomorrow. He had to have some fun in his life, after all.

He realized suddenly that this—the fishing boat, the hours, the drudgery—this *was* his life. It was inconceivable.

## 12:00 p.m.

Nina opened the dryer. "Oh, my God!" she wailed. "More infant sweaters!"

## 1:00 p.m.

Claire was shampooing her hair with mayonnaise, which was kind of gross but sure did make it shiny. She was also practicing smiling in the mirror. She was getting quite good at it.

## 2:00 p.m.

Christopher was doing some landscaping outside Passmores' Restaurant. Every time he threw a shovelful of earth onto a tree's roots, he imagined he was burying Kendra. It helped pass the time.

## 3:00 p.m.

Zoey's roommate, Mary Beth, said, "Have you been

wearing my fuzzy red sweater with the embroidered sunflowers?"

She was serious.

## 4:00 p.m.

Kate woke up from her second nap of the day and decided that she would go to Aaron's show. If she could find something to wear.

## 5:00 p.m.

Aaron was already on the mainland, testing the sound equipment. As he leaned over to plug in an amplifier an idea skittered across the top of his mind. Had he ever given Mia the number at his mom's house? But the thought had no more weight than a water bug speeding across the surface of a lake, and by the time Aaron straightened up again, it was gone.

## 6:00 p.m.

Jake found a letter in his mailbox and read it twice, shaking his head in disbelief.

## 7:00 p.m.

Benjamin was watching the sexy parts of *Striptease*. His thoughts are probably best not recorded.

# Twenty

Kate huddled in the shelter of Jake's arms on the ferry. He rested his chin on the top of her head. Kate watched Claire and Nina and Aisha standing near the railing.

"Hey, remember that guy you called the Snacker?" Nina said.

Aisha laughed. "Of course I do. He stayed all summer long last year, and every single time I went into the kitchen, he was polishing off something or other."

Kate stared at them. How could they be so happy and carefree? Would they talk to her if she joined them? Probably. But she had nothing to say to them. It made her exhausted just thinking about it.

She shivered.

"Cold?" Jake asked.

She nodded wordlessly, and he slipped his jacket around her.

"How are you feeling today?" he asked, rubbing her arms to warm them.

She shrugged.

"Did you start taking the medicine?"

"Sure," Kate lied. "It takes a while to work, though."

"Oh," Jake said. "Listen, what borough of New York does your mom live in?"

"Why do you want to know *that?*"

"Because I want to call her."

"You want to what?" Kate stared at him.

"I want to talk to her," Jake said. "I want to convince her to let you stay. If I can, that'll be one less thing for you to worry about."

"Jake . . ."

"Kate, come on, there aren't that many things I can do to help. Let me do this." He looked at her imploringly.

Kate wavered. "Okay," she said finally. "I'll give you the number tomorrow."

Jake smiled and kissed her.

She was still shivering. "I think I want to go down below for a little while," she said.

"Want some company?"

"No, I—I'll be right back."

She went down onto the lower deck, which was deserted, and sat down on a bench. She felt so cold and so tired. Was there anything worse than being cold and tired all the time?

She pulled her feet under her and slipped her hands into the pockets of Jake's jacket. Something crackled in the left pocket—a folded piece of paper. Kate pulled it out idly and unfolded it. Familiar handwriting leaped out at her, and she began reading with mounting alarm.

*Dear Jake,*

*I do not know if Kate has had the forthrightness to tell you the full story of her condition, but as her mother, I at least feel compelled to do so.*

*For the past few years Kate has suffered from chronic clinical depression. I do not have the time nor space to inform you fully on this disorder, but suffice it to say that it is very serious indeed.*

*I am writing to ask for your help, as Kate is in*

*denial concerning her affliction. She feels she can
handle it herself, but I'm sure you'll agree that
her place is here with me. . . .*

There was more, but Kate didn't read it. Her hands
were shaking too badly. Her mother's phrases were
ringing in her mind. *Kate's affliction . . . this disorder
. . . she is in denial . . .*

And Jake had read this! Jake had read this horrible
garbage! What must he think? He must—

She froze.

*Jake wanted her mother's phone number.*

Everything was suddenly clear to Kate. Jake wanted
her mother's phone number. He said it was to convince
her that Kate would be okay, but of course that's what
he *said*. Obviously what he wanted was to call and dis-
cuss Kate's—Kate's *affliction.*

Kate's hands tightened reflexively, and she crum-
pled the letter. She tried to shred it and only managed
to tear it into three large ragged pieces. Furious, she
threw them aside, wondering who in the world she
could turn to now.

Nina approached Benjamin as he stood in his usual
solitary spot by the railing. "Hi," she said shyly.

"Hi," he answered, smiling.

For a minute neither of them spoke, and then Benjamin reached for her hands. "Have you ever seen the
director's cut of *9½ Weeks*?" he asked.

Nina laced her fingers with his. "No, but I saw
Burke's cut," she said.

"Burke, as in your father?"

She nodded. "He rented it once because he had it
confused with *Six Weeks;* you know, that movie about
the girl with leukemia? Well, anyway, we all sat down

to watch it together, but my dad kept fast-forwarding through all the sex scenes."

Benjamin laughed. "How long was the movie?"

Nina laughed, too. "I don't know. Five, ten minutes?"

Benjamin pulled her closer to him. "Are we friends again?" he asked, kissing her forehead.

"Of course we are," Nina answered.

But she didn't feel like they were friends. She felt like they were cousins, or roommates, or coworkers. People together by circumstance rather than choice.

The ferry pulled up to the Weymouth landing, and Jake checked his watch. Kate was nowhere in sight. He wondered if she had changed her mind about going to the show. Well, if she had, that was okay. He would take her somewhere else, even back home.

The gates clanged down, and passengers began to get off.

"Hey, where's Kate?" Lucas asked.

Jake shrugged uncomfortably. "She was cold and went below," he said. "Why don't you guys go on ahead?"

Lucas looked surprised. "Why? It'll only take a second to go get her."

Jake tried to think of a plausible lie. "She wasn't feeling very good," he said. "Really, you guys go ahead. We'll catch up." He hoped that was true.

"You sure?" Lucas asked, concerned.

Jake nodded.

"Okay, I guess. We'll see you in a couple of minutes." Lucas hurried off the ferry to where Claire and Nina stood waiting for him.

Jake went down to the lower deck. The only person there was a skinny kid who sometimes worked the late shift on the *Minnow*. He was sweeping.

"Hey," Jake said. "Did you see a girl down here?"

The skinny guy leaned on his broom. "Real pretty redhead?"

"Yeah."

"Sure, she was down here, but she's off by now. I saw her waiting right near the gates when we landed."

Jake frowned. Why wouldn't Kate come up on deck and find him? Would she leave without him?

"Thanks," he said to the skinny guy, turning to go. Then something near one of the benches caught his eye. A pile of jagged slips of paper. He went over and picked them up. For a minute he thought his heart had stopped beating.

Kate's mother's letter. Oh, God, had he left that in the pocket of his jacket? Obviously he had, or it wouldn't be here now. He dropped the pieces and ran back up on deck.

"Kate?" he called. He bounded onto the landing. "Kate? Kate!"

He walked quickly up the street. Where would she have gone after reading that horrible letter? Would she have sense enough to know that he didn't believe a word of it? That he wanted to call her mother and tell her what trash he thought it was?

"Kate!" he called again. He was walking faster now, but soon he was running.

# Twenty-one

Claire smiled at the bouncer, a big guy with a blond ponytail. He looked a little disconcerted, but he smiled back. She filed past him with everyone else into the Sand Bar.

She had already smiled dazzlingly at Lucas, Benjamin, and Christopher on the ferry. They had all seemed a little surprised, too. But she was determined. It was part of her plan to smile and flirt with every man in sight. She would show Aaron that she could have any man she wanted.

She was wearing a tight sky blue minidress, and although it was probably a little too elegant for the Sand Bar, Claire liked the way it looked. Men liked the way it looked, too, judging by the fact that some man she didn't even know had given her his business card on the ferry. (Claire had smiled at him, too.)

Aaron's band was playing in a separate room of the Sand Bar, and the others lined up to pay the cover charge. Claire hung back, lingering at the bar. She gave the bartender a seductive smile. "I'd like a ginger ale, please."

"You're not paying these prices for soda, are you?" Nina said from behind her. "Good God, do you know what the markup is? About 750 percent!"

Claire stared at her. "Has Dad taken over your body? Are you going to start talking about interest rates next?"

Nina looked tempted. "Well, actually, savings is always a better bet—"

"Nina, spare me."

"What? I've learned the value of a dollar. You would, too, if you did half the work I do."

"I already know the value of a dollar, Nina," Claire said. "I didn't have to max out Dad's credit card to learn it. Anyway, I'm not about to go thirsty all night just because you're suddenly the penny police." Claire smiled at the bartender again, who had listened patiently to the whole exchange. He moved off to get her drink.

Nina tugged at her sleeve. "You don't have to *buy* a drink," she whispered. "You could have brought your own thermos, like I did."

"Oh, for heaven's sake. That's the dumbest thing I ever heard."

Nina looked offended. "Fine. Ignore my good advice. Drink whatever you want."

"I am!" Claire said, exasperated.

The bartender returned with her ginger ale.

"Can I ask you something?" Nina said.

"I guess."

"Why are you smiling in that creepy way?"

Claire's eyebrows drew together. "It's not creepy; that's just my personality."

Nina let out a howl of laughter. "You said it, not me!" She moved away, still laughing and shaking her head.

Claire waited until Nina had gone into the other room. Then she composed herself, pasted on another smile, and approached the guy taking money and stamping the backs of people's hands.

"Hi," Claire said. "I think my name is on the band's list."

The guy pulled a clipboard off a nail on the wall next to him. "Your name?"

"Mia."

The guy scanned the list. "Mia . . . Mia . . . here you are." He checked off a name.

Claire extended her hand, and he stamped it.

"Enjoy the show, Mia."

"Oh, I will," Claire said. Her smile grew wider. It was almost predatory now.

Zoey had been invited to another cocktail party, but she'd decided not to go. MaryBeth went. She put on a yellow dress with ruffles and tied a big yellow bow in her hair and flounced off to where the bus waited to take all the interns to the hotel.

Zoey watched her go, and then she put on her oldest pair of sweats and the Boston Bruins T-shirt she usually slept in. She grabbed her purse and walked the fourteen blocks to the supermarket.

She was used to the Weymouth supermarket, which was vast and sparkling and not only contained every product you might possibly want but several *varieties* of every product you might possibly want. This Washington, D.C., supermarket was small and cramped and dirty. Zoey took a miniature-size cart and began wheeling slowly up and down the aisles.

She threw a can of ravioli in the cart and then a TV dinner. The youth hostel had a community microwave, and she and MaryBeth had a hot plate in their room.

A bag of chips went into the cart. Zoey sighed. She didn't know what she was hungry for. No, that was wrong—she knew precisely what. She wanted to pad across the kitchen of her own house, open her own refrigerator, take out a container of something brought home from the restaurant—chicken soup, corn fritters, fried calamari, anything—and scamper back to her room, where she could snuggle under the covers with Lucas, feeding him every other bite.

Zoey's eyes stung. She missed Lucas, she missed Nina, she missed Benjamin, her parents, North Harbor, Maine, pine trees, you name it. What was she doing in Washington? Why didn't she just go home? But she couldn't do that. She couldn't admit defeat and scurry back. She couldn't pass up what everyone agreed was a marvelous opportunity. She would have to stay. But Lucas . . . she missed him so much. And she couldn't even call him because during the day he was working and at night he went to bed at seven-thirty.

She wheeled her cart slowly past the freezer section, and the ice cream caught her eye. Zoey had once read a line in a book she remembered well: *Hot fudge fills deep needs*. Well, she would find out if that was true. She hurled a carton of vanilla Breyers in the cart and went in search of hot fudge sauce.

A minute later she was wheeling her cart up to the cash register. She watched in some amazement as the cashier rang up her purchase. Was she really going to go home and eat all this junk?

"Fourteen-oh-seven," the cashier said.

Zoey reached for her purse and stopped. She patted her hips in sudden panic, checked her shoulder for the strap, frantically scrambled her hands into the corners of her cart. But it was no use. Her purse was gone.

Aaron was up onstage when Claire came in. He smiled at her. God, she looked great. Every guy in the room was probably ogling her. She said she didn't like that, but then why did she dress that way?

She came over and stood next to the stage, smiling at the other band members and greeting them all by name. She looked at him last, ducking her head and looking almost shy. She shifted from foot to foot, and her figure was even more clearly outlined. All four other band members breathed more heavily.

Aaron jumped down from the stage and kissed her quickly. He steered her away from the stage and kissed her more slowly. "You look incredible."

She gave him a mockingly modest look. "Aw, thanks, sweetie."

"I mean it."

She glanced around. "When do you start?"

He tried to put his arms around her again. "Not for a while."

She disentangled herself. "I have to go to the ladies' room, but I'll see you before you go on."

He let her go reluctantly. "Hurry back."

She smiled at him over her shoulder.

An alarm bell in the back of Aaron's mind began ringing. Claire was smiling a lot. But maybe that didn't mean anything. He would have to find Mia and tell her that he didn't have time for her. He'd say that he was always nervous and keyed up at shows and needed to be left alone. Anyway, Mia knew he saw other people, right? He was always telling her that.

Aaron was sure he had it all under control.

# Twenty-two

Claire didn't really have to go to the bathroom. She only said that because she wanted to stop kissing Aaron. But then she decided she might as well. The lines would be longer later, and the blue minidress was so formfitting that it took some getting in and out of.

And so it happened that she was in a stall, smoothing the dress back down over her hips, when she heard it—*that voice.* She would have known it anywhere, of course. The phone message was seared into her memory. Bright, chirpy, flirtatious, *pert:* It was Mia.

And it wasn't hard for Claire to recognize her since Mia was out there chattering at the top of her voice about Aaron. Claire finished adjusting her dress and listened.

"Oh, thanks," Mia was saying. "Well, Aaron likes the color. . . . No, I haven't heard the band, but everyone says they're great."

Mia's friend was farther away, near the door of the bathroom, and Claire could barely make out her voice. "You and Aaron going to do something after the show?"

"Well, of course," Mia said.

"Don't leave without saying good-bye to me," the friend said.

"I won't," Mia called, and Claire heard the noise of the bathroom door swinging shut.

She opened the door of her stall and stepped out. Mia was standing at the sink. She wore a clingy lime green shirt that emphasized her full breasts, and her cutoff shorts showed lean, strong legs. She had huge dark eyes, dark skin, and jutting cheekbones.

*Why am I surprised?* Claire thought. *I know what type Aaron likes. I know it better than most people.*

Mia was fluffing out her hair in the mirror. Claire continued to study her. She had nice hair, dark and straight. Claire wondered suddenly if the comment about Aaron liking the color referred to Mia's shirt or Mia's hair. Maybe that wasn't her natural hair color. But that didn't make it any less pretty. Besides, Claire thought, all girls use bottled gunk of one kind or another on their hair.

She herself had just this afternoon put *mayonnaise* on her hair. And it was well worth it, she decided, glancing at her own reflection. Her hair fell in perfect shiny waves to her shoulders. She didn't bother to check her makeup. Claire's makeup was always flawless.

"Excuse me," she said to Mia.

Mia was apparently about to leave. "Yes?" she said pleasantly. She had a small, elfin face with even features.

Claire tried to make herself blush. "I couldn't help overhearing just now," she said. "Is your boyfriend in the band?"

Mia's face glowed with pleasure. "Yes, he is. His name is Aaron Mendel."

"I'm afraid I don't know which one he is," Claire said regretfully.

"Oh, I'm sure you do," Mia said. "He's the tall one, with the dark curly hair and the blue eyes?"

"You're kidding!" Claire gasped. "He's so hand-some. You're very lucky."

Mia smiled modestly. "I know."

"Have you been going out for a long time?"

Mia hesitated. Claire was satisfied to see that she had Mia rattled. Mia didn't want to admit to some strange beautiful girl that she'd only been out with Aaron a few times. "Sort of," Mia hedged finally.

Claire smiled encouragingly. "Well, you make a stunning couple," she said generously. "You must be very serious."

"Oh, we are," Mia said. She looked so happy, Claire almost felt bad. "We're very—" She paused and took a breath. "We're very much in love."

"That's wonderful," Claire said. "Do you—well, this is going to sound strange, but—could you introduce me? I—I have a crush on one of the other guys."

She was proud of this final invention, which had come to her out of nowhere. It certainly did the trick with Mia. Her face cleared of doubt instantly. "Oh, of course," she said. "Which one?"

"I—I'd rather not say."

"I understand," Mia said. "Well, come on, let's go find Aaron."

Claire summoned up one more smile. She knew it would be her last this evening. "Yes," she said. "Let's."


Lucas leaned against the bar, trying to appear lost in thought. He felt so conspicuously alone. Everyone else seemed to have some secret agenda and had peeled off the instant they reached the Sand Bar. The only ones he could even see anymore were Aaron up onstage and Aisha and Kendra. He supposed he could go horn in on their conversation. But that wasn't what he wanted. He wanted a conversation of his own, preferably with

Zoey. He missed her so much. With Zoey around he always felt like he *belonged*. And belonging was not a feeling Lucas had ever had much experience with before.

He was trying so hard to project a don't-bother-me-I'm-having-deep-important-thoughts appearance that he was almost surprised when someone tapped him on the arm. "Hey," Nina said. "Want to come to the store with me?"

Lucas shook himself out of his daze. "What store?"

"The 7-Eleven. I need to refill my thermos." She held up the silver thermos to show him.

"Nina, for God's sake, let me buy you a Coke—"

"No, a penny saved is a penny earned," Nina said. "Are you coming or not?"

"Only if you promise not say things like, *A penny saved is a penny earned.*"

Nina laughed. "It's a deal," she said. Lucas thought she looked pretty, or as pretty as she could with her bangs gone. She was wearing cutoffs and a gold velvet shirt with huge bell sleeves. The shirt was so ancient that the velvet was threadbare in places.

They left the Sand Bar and walked out into the twilight. Lucas studied the sky for a moment. "So," he said. "Do you have any stories for me about convenience stores?"

"Stories?" Nina repeated, puzzled.

"Yeah, you always have some story or anecdote about whatever we happen to be doing."

"I do?" Nina looked pleased, like he had just paid her a huge compliment. "Well, gosh, the pressure's on now. Let me think. . . . Okay, once when we were on vacation in Montana, we stopped at a convenience store and I tried to order a large Coke and the guy wouldn't give it to me unless I called it a Big Hoss."

Lucas laughed, and Nina smiled delightedly. "I didn't think anyone would ever think that funny but me," she said. "I mean, at the time Claire was in hysterics, but it wasn't the same—" She interrupted herself with a little gasp. "Oh, Lucas, look!"

She knelt down and picked something off the sidewalk. She brushed it off and held it out for him to see. It was a ring with a large solitaire diamond. An engagement ring.

"Oh, it's so pretty," Nina said sorrowfully. "Whoever lost this is going to be so upset."

Lucas was surprised. He had never heard Nina admire a piece of clothing or jewelry. In fact, he didn't think he'd ever seen her wear a piece of jewelry. "I don't think it's real," he said. "If it were real, it would be worth thousands. It's probably from a gum ball machine."

Nina still seemed in awe of the ring. "That doesn't make it any less beautiful," she said. She slipped it on her finger—her left hand, Lucas noticed. He wondered if she was thinking of Benjamin. They were quiet the rest of the way to the 7-Eleven.

Nina took a bottle of diet Coke up to the counter.

"That'll be a dollar twenty," the man said.

Nina paid him. Then she poured the Coke into her thermos and gave the man the bottle back. "I'd like the deposit, please."

The man rolled his eyes, and for an awful moment Lucas feared Nina would rattle off some money-related proverb, but just then a couple hurried into the 7-Eleven.

The woman was almost in tears. "It's no use," she said to the man. "I would have heard it drop if it fell off in here. Oh, it's all my fault!"

"Now, Helen," the man said reassuringly. "Let's at least take a look around."

Helen appeared not to have heard him. She was about thirty-five and very pretty, with long dark hair pulled into a bun. "All my fault," she repeated. "I should have had it resized a long time ago."

At the word *resized,* Nina's ears perked up. "Resized?" she said. "Are you the ones who lost this ring?" She extended her hand toward them like a new bride. The ring sparkled in the fluorescent lighting.

"Oh!" Helen cried. "Oh, my God! Where did you find it?"

"On the sidewalk, just outside," Nina said, pulling the ring off and handing it unceremoniously to Helen.

Helen slipped it on her own finger reverently. "Oh, thank you so much," she breathed. She leaned over and hugged Nina impulsively. "Thank you, my dear."

Lucas was watching Helen's husband, who had taken out his wallet. He appeared to be sizing up Nina, taking in the old shorts, the frayed shirt, the inexpert haircut.

*Wouldn't he be surprised to know she's Burke Geiger's daughter,* Lucas thought.

Helen's husband opened his wallet. "Can I offer you a reward?" he asked Nina gently.

Helen nodded. "Oh, yes! Of course she must have a reward. Please, you must take it," she said to Nina, who, as a matter of fact, had shown no sign of refusing it.

Helen's husband looked thoughtful. "How does three hundred dollars sound?"

Nina's eyes were shining. Helen and her husband probably thought it was because she'd never had that much money before in her life. Lucas knew it was about the same amount of money she owed her father.

Helen's husband counted out the money and handed Nina a pile of crisp twenties.

"Oh, thank you," Nina breathed.

She hugged Helen's husband, and then she hugged Helen again. Helen's husband shook hands with Lucas, even though he hadn't even done anything. Even the man behind the counter looked a little misty-eyed.

And then Nina threw her arms around Lucas. "Isn't this perfect?" she whispered in his ear. "I won't have to make all the beds anymore and—Lucas, won't this make a wonderful story?"

Lucas couldn't answer. He had realized two things at once. One, that no one had hugged him since Zoey left. Two, that Nina's hair smelled like violets: sweet, incredible, so real it made you emotional, even though you knew it was just her shampoo.

# Twenty-three

Aisha and Kendra settled themselves at the table while Christopher went to the bar to get their drinks. Aisha smiled at him as he walked away. He was being a good sport about Kendra coming along. Aisha herself was glad Kendra had come because she was clearly so excited about it.

"Oh, look," Kendra said, practically bouncing in her chair. "There's Aaron onstage! He's waving at us."

Aisha laughed. "He's not a rock star, at least not yet," she said.

"I know, but it's still exciting."

Aisha glanced across the table. Kendra looked so pretty in white silk pants and a bright pink halter. She looked young and fresh and lovely—and yet Aisha felt the same finger of fear on her spine as she had that morning. *She knows something.* Aisha turned that idea over in her mind. Why did she feel that?

*Because it's true,* her mind answered.

Yes, it was undoubtedly true. Aisha trusted her own instincts. And yet Kendra seemed so innocent. What kind of deep, dark secret could she have?

*Maybe it's not about her. Maybe it's about you.*

Aisha thought about the conversation she had overheard between Kendra and Christopher. *Aisha must never know.* What—

"Hey, Eesh," Kendra said, interrupting her thoughts. "I found something today to show you."

Aisha tried to quiet the voice in her head. "Really? What?"

Kendra pulled a photograph out of her pocket. "A picture of Christopher when he was seventeen," she said, giggling. "You won't believe the hair. It's like the Jackson Five all rolled into one person."

Aisha laughed and held out her hand, but before she could touch the photograph, there was a loud crash and Christopher stood next to them in a small sea of broken glass and dripping soda.

"My pants!" Kendra wailed, jumping to her feet. Her white pants were spattered with syrupy brown stains. Aisha's own feet and legs were dry.

Christopher grabbed Kendra's arm, and even from her chair Aisha could see his fingers digging into her flesh. "What the hell are you doing?" he barked. He shook the photograph in front of her face.

"Hey," Aisha began softly. She pushed back her chair, but they paid no attention to her.

"It's just a picture!" Kendra cried. "Just a dumb picture! Why are you so paranoid?" She broke free from his grip and ran toward the ladies' room. Christopher cursed under his breath and followed her.

Aisha sat alone at the table. A waitress came to mop up the mess. Aisha was glad that even preband, the bar was noisy enough that no one noticed the fight. She took the dishrag the waitress offered her and began wiping the table.

The photograph had been dropped and was lying in a pool of Coke. She picked it up carefully and dried it with the cloth. It showed Christopher—such a young Christopher!—in a white tuxedo. Aisha smiled faintly. He did have a lot of hair, and it was awfully styled-looking hair. *More awful than styled,* she thought wryly.

But mainly it was his expression that interested her. Was this her Christopher smiling so widely and openly at the camera? Where was the reserve and the restraint and coolness she knew so well? What had happened to make this laughing boy so serious?

She slipped the picture into her purse. Then she paused and pulled it back out. Christopher was wearing a tuxedo. Not a baby blue one, but a white one. But both Christopher and Kendra had told her that their school didn't have proms or homecomings or anything like that.

A small straight line appeared between Aisha's eyebrows. Why would Christopher be wearing a tux?


Claire followed Mia through the crowd to the stage. She wasn't surprised to see that Mia had a springy, energetic walk. Claire trailed behind more slowly. Now that she wasn't smiling anymore, her face was calm and beautiful, and cold.

Up onstage Aaron saw them coming toward him, and Claire was faintly pleased to see that he had the good grace (and the good sense) to look terrified.

"Aaron!" Mia called happily. "Come on down; I want you to meet someone."

Aaron hesitated. Claire wondered if he was mentally calculating the distance to his car. But in the end he came down from the stage.

"Aaron," Mia said. "I want you to meet—gosh, I'm sorry, I don't even know your name."

"Aaron already knows my name," Claire said smoothly.

"He does?" Mia said. "But in the bathroom you—*do* you know her?" she asked, turning to Aaron.

Aaron was looking at Claire. She could see from his face that he was frantically searching for a way out. He wasn't quite ready to admit that the gig was up. But then he seemed to make some sort of decision. "Yes, I know her," he said.

Claire wondered fleetingly what he would say. *She's my stepsister? She's my cousin? She's a madwoman?*

Aaron cleared his throat. "She's my girlfriend," he said clearly, scoring his one (and only) point with Claire for the evening.

"Girlfriend?" Mia repeated, dismayed. She glanced from Claire to Aaron, but they were looking at each other.

"So imagine my surprise when Mia told me she was your girlfriend," Claire said coolly.

"Girlfriend?" Aaron nearly squeaked.

"And that you were very much in love."

"In love?" Aaron squeaked again, sounding like a parrot.

Mia looked confused and hurt by Claire's defection. "I didn't—"

"Please excuse us," Claire said. "Aaron and I need to talk outside."

She turned and walked through the crowd again and out the back door. She didn't turn until she was standing outside, next to a Dumpster. Aaron was right behind her.

"Claire," he said immediately. "You have to believe me, I'm not in love with Mia."

Claire was surprised. It had never occurred to her that he was. "That's not the point," she said.

Aaron looked wary. "It's not?"

"No. The point is that you told me that you weren't going to see her again. And obviously you've seen her enough for *Mia* to be very much in love, even if you're not."

"I've—I've only seen her a couple of times—"

"That's a couple of more times than we agreed to,"

Claire said. "It was going to be *one* date, remember? One date for each of us, to make Burke and Sarah happy." She had to stop talking. Her voice was starting to quaver.

Aaron didn't notice. "I just invited her here so there would be a bigger crowd. I—"

Fury made Claire's voice stronger. "Don't lie. Her name was on the guest list."

Aaron blanched. Claire knew more than he thought. *But do I know everything?* she wondered.

Aaron ran a hand through his hair. "Okay," he said at last. "Her name was on the guest list. I admit it. But—Claire, I love you."

She raised an eyebrow.

"I do," Aaron said. "Are we going to break up? After all we've been through? Over *Mia?*"

Claire was silent. Did she want to break up with Aaron? Did she want to lose him again? Why had she gotten all dressed up and come here tonight if not to fight for him?

"That's up to you," she said at last.

"What do you mean?"

"The world is full of Mias," Claire said. "Can you promise me that you'll give this one up? And the next one? And the one after that?"

Aaron hesitated.

It was unbelievable, but he hesitated. It wasn't very long, but Claire imagined she could feel the planet turning slowly while she waited for him to speak.

"Of course I can—" he began, but she cut him off.

"Your silence is very articulate."

"Claire—"

She turned and began walking. As she passed the doorway she noticed Mia silhouetted there. Claire didn't care. She was finished with Mia. She was finished with both of them.

# Twenty-four

Kate threw a half-used bottle of mouthwash in the suitcase. She glanced wide-eyed around her room. What else could she possibly take? The suitcase was already full of cameras and rolls of film. She opened a drawer at random and added a heavy wool sweater to the pile.

Her mind wouldn't stop chattering away at full speed. It was monotonous and loud and rapid, like the sound of a train. *canItrustJakewhydid Motherwritethat Iwillnevergobacktohernowbutwherecan Igo—*

On and on it went during her flight from the ferry, during her water taxi ride back, as she fled up the stairs to her room.

The stream of thoughts distracted her, kept her from thinking clearly. Where was she going to go? To New York? To her *mother?* She looked at the suitcase suddenly and saw that it looked like it had been packed by a band of monkeys. Sweater sleeves dangled out the sides, her camera wasn't even in its case, on the top was a single pink-foam hair curler.

Kate burst into tears. How was she going to run away if she couldn't even pack a bag? She was worn out and confused. Why did Jake talk about helping her and then not even tell her about the letter? Why did he sometimes say he wanted her to stay and other times seem so unsure?

She wiped her eyes with the back of her hand. She wanted to crawl into her bed, but the stupid suitcase was on it, and she felt too weary to move it. Instead she dropped to her knees and crawled between the mattress and the box spring. She liked the weight of the mattress on top of her.

"Oh, Jake," she whispered softly. "Oh, Jake."

Then she closed her eyes and, by force of will, plunged herself into oblivion.

"You don't understand," Zoey practically wailed at the policeman. She was sitting with him in the wire cage next to the supermarket manager's office. "My whole entire *life* was in that purse."

The policeman looked at her gravely. "We'll do our best, ma'am."

Zoey didn't like him calling her *ma'am.* That sounded too grown-up, as if he expected her to be all calm and responsible and independent. She wanted him to call her Zoey, she wanted her father, she wanted Lucas.

"My entire life," she repeated. "My wallet, my cash, my credit card, my keys, my driver's license, everything!" Zoey's voice had been rising dangerously, and suddenly it cracked and she was on the brink of tears.

She was vaguely aware of people watching her. *Oh, great,* she realized. *They probably think I've been caught shoplifting and that's why I'm up in this cage, wailing.*

"Ma'am, ma'am," the policeman said, clearly dismayed. "No need to cry."

"There is too a need to cry!" Zoey practically yelled. Her tears retreated a little. "If there was *ever* a need to cry, it's right now."

161

The policeman handed her a Kleenex. She blew her nose. "Can I use that phone?"

The policeman looked relieved. He'd probably thought she would cry and throw herself into his arms or something. "Sure," he said, indicating the ancient black phone next to him.

Zoey picked up the receiver and turned her back on the policeman. She dialed Lucas's number and then her father's credit card number. She glanced at her watch. Nine o'clock. Lucas would be asleep, but—she needed him. She needed to hear his voice.

The phone began ringing.

"Hello?" It was Lucas's mother.

"Mrs. Cabral? This is Zoey. . . ." She waited, but Mrs. Cabral didn't say anything else. No surprise there. "Anyway, I know Lucas is sleeping, but could you please wake him? It's important."

"He's not sleeping," Mrs. Cabral said. "He's off at some bar with that girl."

"Girl?"

"Yes, that Nora or Nina or whoever he's always calling. Call him tomorrow."

"Mrs. Cabral—" Zoey began, but the hum of a dial tone cut her off. Mrs. Cabral had hung up.

Zoey began dialing again, this time her own home number. She could barely see to hit the numbers. She was crying too hard.


Nina searched the Sand Bar and finally found Benjamin out back, leaning against the tall wooden fence at the edge of the lot.

"Benjamin!" she called. She threw her arms around his waist. "You won't believe what happened. I found this woman's ring, and she and her husband gave me a three-hundred-dollar reward, and I can stop doing laundry, which means my dad can stop wearing pink underwear and—and—isn't it great?" she finished lamely. Benjamin didn't look all that amazed.

"That's wonderful," he said, putting an arm around her shoulders.

She took his hand. "Well, come on back inside, and I'll buy you a drink. I'll buy you ten drinks."

Benjamin didn't allow her to pull him toward the bar. "Neen, I was actually just thinking about leaving."

"Leaving?" Nina said, dismayed. "We just got here! The band hasn't even started." She noticed that he didn't say where he was going—and he didn't invite her to join him.

"I know," Benjamin said soothingly. "But I'm restless."

"But you're the only reason I came here tonight," Nina said plaintively.

"Well, then you shouldn't have come." Her heart must have been plainly upon her face, because he softened. "I don't mean that like it sounds," he said. "It's just everyone is putting so much pressure on me to do what they want—"

"By *everyone* do you mean me?" Nina asked bitterly.

"No, I mean everyone: my parents, Zoey, my friends, but yes, you, too." Benjamin looked distant. "I spent so much time not being able to do anything but what other people wanted—"

"And now you don't want to do anything that someone else might want you to do."

"Nina, don't be unfair," he pleaded. "I still love you."

"*Still!*" Nina's voice was full of tears.

He grimaced. "Look, tonight is just a bad night. Let's talk tomorrow." He tried to put his arm around her again.

But Nina shook her head. "Tonight is no different from any other night," she said softly. "And tomorrow isn't going to be any better." She took a deep breath. "I don't think we should see each other anymore."

"Nina, don't be so extreme. That's not what I want."

"Well, maybe it's what I want, Benjamin!" she flared. "Did you ever think of that? Did you ever, for one second, think what it does to me to feel the way you make me feel?"

He studied her in his old, maddeningly calm way. "What way is that?"

Nina threw up her hands. "Like—like some little yapping dog, clutching at your pant leg and saying, 'Pay attention to me!' It's horrible."

"Oh, Nina." He pulled her into his arms and buried his lips in her hair.

She put her hands against his chest. "I can't go on like this. I really can't."

He stroked her back gently. "I know."

She was crying softly. He held her for a while, and then she pushed herself away and wiped her nose on one of her bell sleeves. "I'm sorry, Benjamin," she said. "But we can't see each other anymore."

"I'm sorry, too," he said. "I wish it could different."

Nina said nothing because it could be different. But it wasn't.

# Twenty-five

Claire strode through the parking lot, hating the way the tight minidress kept her from running. An hour ago the dress had been a joy to wear: seductive, alluring, eye-catching. Now it was only uncomfortable and tacky. Claire couldn't wait to change out of it. She wanted to go home and wash off all her makeup and sit on the roof and study the weather conditions. Weather was so interesting and powerful and could certainly hurt you, but it would never break your heart.

"Hey," a voice behind her said. "Hey, wait up."

Claire didn't even slow down, but because she was wearing that damn skirt, the bouncer easily caught up with her. It was the same guy from before, with the blond ponytail.

"Hey," he said. "I have something for you." He held out an envelope. Claire didn't take it. "It's not from me," the bouncer said. "Someone else gave it to me. Said it was for the beautiful dark-haired girl in the blue dress." He smiled at her.

Claire supposed he remembered her smile from earlier, but he wasn't getting another one. She snatched the letter from him without a word. Probably some stupid, obnoxious, leering letter from one of the stupid,

165

obnoxious, leering men she had smiled at. She kept walking.

"Bye," the bouncer called sarcastically. "Have a good night."

Claire ignored him. She ripped open the envelope, throwing it on the ground. Inside was a stack of photographs, held together by a rubber band. Claire's fingers went numb, and she almost dropped them. She hadn't been expecting this.

She stood under a streetlight and removed the rubber band. She looked at the top photo, and then the one beneath it, and then the next. Each one was more in focus. She flipped through them faster and faster, mindless of the few that fell to the pavement, until she held the final one in her hand.

She knew at last what was in the snapshots. The rectangular glowing shape was a window, probably at night, because it was filled with warm light. In the center of the window was a girl with her back to the camera. She was naked, and her arms were above her head. She was gathering her hair into a knot on the top of her head, probably before getting into the bathtub.

Before terror overtook her, some very small part of Claire's mind informed her that the picture must have been taken with a telephoto lens because her bedroom was on the third floor, and the girl in the picture was her.

Christopher threw open the bathroom door so hard, it dented the wall. Kendra looked up from the sink, where she was dabbing at her ruined pants with a wet paper towel.

No one else was in the bathroom, but Christopher wouldn't have cared if there were twenty nuns changing clothes. He crossed the floor in two bounds and seized Kendra's narrow shoulders in his large hands and shook her.

"What do you think you're doing?" he shouted. "I won't let you do this to me! Do you understand? Do you? Do you get it?"

He was still shaking her, and he shook her harder with every word. Her head snapped back and forth, and her hair tumbled into her face. She didn't answer him. Probably she was too scared.

Abruptly Christopher released her, and she collapsed against the sink, the damp paper towel still in her hand. He had to shove his hands into his pockets to keep from shaking her again.

"This is it, Kendra," he said in a more controlled way. "You are getting on a bus for Boston—or anywhere else—tomorrow."

Kendra pushed her hair back with an unsteady hand. "Aisha wanted to see a picture," she said. "I was just showing her—"

"Jesus!" Christopher shouted. "So you show her *that* picture?" He couldn't even look at her, he was so furious.

"It was the only one I had," Kendra protested. "Aisha didn't know what it was, Christopher. You can't tell it's a wedding picture."

At the word *wedding* Christopher felt all the anger drain out of him, leaving only slick, hollow fear. His mouth felt full of pennies. Until that moment he hadn't known what people meant when they said *the coppery taste of fear.*

Kendra evidently thought his silence meant he was willing to listen. She laid a placating hand on his arm. "I like Aisha, Christopher. I like her a lot. I don't want to hurt her. I would never tell her that you were married before."

# Making Out:
## Always loving Zoey

Book 22 in the explosive series about broken hearts, secrets, friendship, and of course, love.

**Lucas** fears he's losing **Zoey**, so he confides in **Nina** who's breaking up with **Ben**. But **Ben's** getting closer to **Lara** who's got plans for **Zoey** that could ruin **Lucas's** life. There's only one thing **Lucas** knows for sure. Whatever happens, he is . . .

## Always loving Zoey